HELLISH INC.

David Adamson

ORIENTATION
MISSION
LOYALTY
STRENGTH
LOYALTY
ENTRANCE

ACKNOWLEDGEMENTS

I want to thank some important people in my life:

My oldest son Samuel

My daughter Jasmine

My youngest son Joshua

A friend who tirelessly listened to me in my darkest moments: "Aaron Webb".

Lastly, I want to say thanks to the spirit that moved me to write.

PROLOGUE

Locked up for eternity.

I am in chains, locked in a cell with only the light shining from one barred window. All at once the heavy door to my cell thrusts open. My master has brought two more specimens. They are tossed carelessly into my grasp, a man and woman. Naked. Bruised. Bloodied. Scared. I strike the man, nearly knocking the life out of him. I grasp the woman and throw her onto my bed. She looks horrified. I don't see her. I don't see the life she once had. I don't feel her pain; I don't sense her passion. I shove a strong sharp-clawed hand into her chest. The light goes out of her eyes. I Howl! I pull from her chest her beating heart. It stops beating, I rip it open. That hurts me! I reach inside and fix the mistake that was made. That hurts me! I close the heart with needle and thread. That scares me! The sewing resembles writing. I thrust the heart back into her chest. I need a rib, so I now kill the man for his rib to fix her chest and close it. I strike her chest so! The heart starts to beat again. I fall to the floor exhausted and await her life to return. Her eyes open. That scares me! Then the light returns to her eyes. That scares her! She screams and jumps up. She doesn't see me! She runs to the window. I cannot reach; my master made the chains too short! A beautiful bird sees her, she clings to it, and it lifts her to heavens.

Now I scream. I wail; I beat my fists onto my bed where she once lay. Her world shakes and moves to the beat of my fists, but she thinks not of me, nor of my repair. I become exhausted. I fall to sleep on my bed. When I awake the man is gone. I am sitting in my cell. I am in chains, in my cell. All at once the heavy door to my cell is thrust open. My master has brought me two more specimens. I am locked up for eternity.

Lightning spills out across the blackened sky. A million tiny lights appear in the wake of the great spark. Eyes, every one of them. Ghostly figures moving to and fro. Lightning again on the left clearly defining the outline of a *Hell's Angel*. The steam drifts from him. His blackened soul steals the light from my sight. As do all the other *Hell's Angels* that are now filling the sky above Earth. There is a fierce pull on the atmosphere, everywhere in the sky, and like a bubble bursting. A crack in the very air, in front of me opens. Without effort, an *Angel of Heaven* steps out. The atmosphere shuts behind her. The realization is immediate. The darkened sky is full of *Hell's Angels*, full of *Angels from Heaven*. It is the most unbelievable sight, the Earth has been a witness to, Ever. And <u>**Evermore**</u>, there will be a battle till the end.

The Angels from Heaven are impossible to look upon. God's power is in their wings. Every move is effortless, their armor is God's own pure love. Their sword and shield appear as lightning and water. Long blonde hair stream from their heads, beautiful faces all, eyes of blue diamond. The Hell's Angels emit only steam and smoke. There is a strange bluish vapor leaking from their eyes. Eyes of the blackest coal. Their wings have the power of *HELL!* The skin encrusted on their body was *Baked* on, when first created in the fires of Hell. They have *No* Need of armor. The darkened sky, now full of Angels. *God's* Angels, *Hell's* Angels, too numerous to count. The feeling is, there are more of them, than all of the grains of sand, on all the beaches on the Earth. *The Most Impressive Sight* ever assembled.

The reason: me. My failed attempt to save one Angel of God, thousands of years ago. I am a **Hell's Angel**. I am **Made** of hate. *Thine* own soul burns in Hell fire, amongst so many others in my Skull. I envisioned the beginning of a way to find acceptance in the sight of God. I ended up being hunted, by both Heaven, *and* Hell. Hunted by Hell Hounds, and every Angel God could send. I found out stealing some of Gods power, creates a vacuum in both heaven and hell. The vacuum opens a *portal* between them, and thus Man, was able to finally glimpse what he was never supposed to envision. Man's armies probed and struck out in all manner of transport into heaven and hell, causing every covenant ever proclaimed by God to be rescinded. So, here we are, looking at every Angel ever made by the heart of **God**, and those *forged* in the fires of **Hell**.

I *hang* in the air effortlessly. A vapor emitted *from* my eyes, allows me to see clearly in the dark, as through it were brightest day. Steam and smoke drift from my body. Water, nor any *gas or particulates may* settle upon my flesh. It has been burned and charred by the fires of Hell. Tiny particles in the air burn off of me as a result, they ignite, and wisps of smoke and steam drift. I hate *all* this world, *all* that are alive, *all* that are the *dead*, saved, or lost. I hate myself. Sometimes I strike my own *Hellish* body, opening a wound that would kill anything! It doesn't kill me! I'm **fuck'n** dead, Dead to the world, Dead to God, Dead to Hell; I'm fuck'n Dead to Me. I'm so goddamn dead, the Dead in Hell *Fear* me! When I move through Hell, the dead lost souls moan at my sight, and cower. I hate them, I hate Hell, I hate myself. I fly up towards the smoke and orange tinted atmosphere of Hell. My wings flash, a portal opens, I slip through.

Hell can't hold me! My wings have a power no Hell hound, or Angel from God can catch, or escape. I use this power to confuse, and distract all in heaven, on earth, or even, in Hell. If I meet an Angel from Heaven, I scream and fly at it! God has made the wings on every angel from heaven indestructible. However, the angel itself can be killed if I am skillful enough. The twist in all of this is that everyone of us have an Angel, to offer protection from attack. This is why when we fight, we fight as *two* always. The fight is twice as dangerous for both Heaven and Hell. God's Angel wings are indestructible, a Hell's Angel's wings are able to teleport through a portal between Hell and Heaven, anywhere, anytime, instantly, thus enabling me to avoid almost any attack. It's Fucking Amazing!!! Mostly, I like to tangle with an Angel, then disappear, reappear, and nearly kill it! Just for *shits n' giggles. I'm Fucking **Dead**, remember? I get being dead. Now, *it's everyone else's turn to get it.*

I cross over from Hell to the Earth. The portal opens, I drift out. The portal shuts. Nothing can get in or out through it, except a *Hell's Angel.* When I glimpse my protector Angel, I try to kill the fuck'n thing! For real, it had better be able to withstand my abuse, or God's Angels will surely end it. I drift through the dark night sky over a city of at least a half a million people. What the fuck! It's Kandahar. These people are always at war. The armies of man move back and forth across the desert, and in the mountainous areas. They kill each other here, year after year, for thousands of years. Man, his power, his arrogance, his greed, and his lust. What a tool in the hands of an Angel of Hell. When **Evermore** arrives and *The Angels of* **Babylon** rise, all Man's power will be swept away, as easily as kicking apart a campfire. Man's power has always been an illusion in order to capture as many souls from God as possible. Fuck man! Fuck God! Fuck me! I'm going to kill something tonight!!

Smoke and steam drift from me! I can see for over 500 miles in any direction. The vapor pouring from my eyes would kill any man, but it enables me to see. It protects my eyes from Hell Fire, and *God's*, *Angel's* armor. Just the glistening from God's pure love off an Angel will blind *anything*, except me. A Hellhound, a Fury, a Demon—all fucking useless against the armor. I see I have company: another Hell's Angel. It floats off to my right and lower. If I can't find what I'm looking for, I will settle for killing that fuck'n thing. We fight together, we fight each other, *We Fight for Hell*. Wait, the atmosphere is pulling at us, this is the sign I've been waiting for. A large bubble emerges, the air splits, the noise is deafening. Out steps 14 of God's Angels. The atmosphere snaps shut; they *hang* in the air effortlessly. This is the going to be a good fuck'n fight; this is going to test that thing down there and our protector Angels. Hell, and Heaven are going to feel pain tonight. I guarantee it. I hate those people down there; I hate those Angels; I hate myself. I'm going to kill everything here tonight, even if I must kill myself to get it done. I've been a **Fixer** for Hell for a long time. If I've got to be replaced, Hell is going to rebel against Earth and Heaven.

Angels from God have eyes of the best **<u>Blue Diamond</u>**. Their *golden* hair streams from each of their heads, like golden silk, long exceptionally fine threads of gold. God's armor is all about an Angel from head to toe. Here and there, there are beads of *Holy Water*; their hands have a white silk glove. Their feet have a thin sheep skin slipper. The sword is as a bolt of lightning. The shield is a portal constructed by God to hold an endless supply of saltwater. A Hell's Angel cannot penetrate it no matter how he tries. The sword can cut limbs off with a single blow or completely gut the thing with a skillful twist in flight. The wings on an Angel of God are indestructible and can serve as an added shield from a portal shifting Hell's Angel. When an Angel of God is killed, the bolt of lightning strikes out across the sky. The portal of saltwater collapses, the water pours from the sky as rain, trying to do as much damage to any Hell's Angel in the area. But however: the wings remain with the Angel for a few seconds. They have a sort of "GPS", that allows God to know precisely where the Angel is, and/or where it died. God reaches across the expanses and touches the dead Angel, the wings disappear. The power is returned to

God. The dead Angel then drifts to the Heavens to appear as a faint star, becoming part of what was, what is, and what will be. This is why, when drops of saltwater fall, they are tears from God.

06/05/16 14:00

God wasn't fooling around when he designed me, God's love is so powerful it can reach into the *heart* of a Hellhound, causing a pain so great in the beast its eyes change color, its hair to lay flat on the back of its neck. The rage goes out of the thing, changing it into a tiger. To *become* a beast that protects its *pride*, forever. I am beautiful to look upon, my hair is made of golden strands, so long it nearly reaches my knees. The golden strands are forged from the very streets in Heaven. A place where all the souls that walk upon the streets, come into contact first, and last, with Heaven. My skin is so smooth and silky that it makes milk, whenever someone touches it. My eyes are made of Blue Diamond, the *truest* diamond ever. So, because of copper, the only metal used in the coloring of the diamond. Copper was first forged by man with gold. Copper looks just as lustrous as gold, but you must continuously polish it without stopping to keep it's shine. Gold on the other hand, polishes to a shine, looks just as attractive years later, as when first polished. Both are heavy, both are soft to touch, but copper was first used to kill as a weapon. Gold was first used to lure someone, by its beauty, and then killed by the weapon copper. Blue diamond eyes can see everything in heaven, on Earth, or in Hell. My blue diamond eyes can see over 500 miles, in every direction. In darkness, smoke, and in Hell. I can tell your truest intentions. I can feel every fiber of your being; I can look into your heart. Touch your pain and absorb it.

Standing here, just after I stepped through a portal from Heaven. The atmosphere snapped shut behind me. I hang effortlessly, the air all around me is filled with a sharp tension, never felt by any Angel from Heaven. I gaze all around my position, Angels everywhere! OH My God, this cannot be! Before me, an Angel from Hell, smoke and steam drift from him. But what, the air is full of them! Full of God's Angels, Full of Hell's Angels! Oh my God, I can see into the heart of a Hell's Angel. This is dangerous, the hate, the rage, the pain, the suffering! The hate, I have never felt hate like this. I didn't know there was hate like this. God never told me about this hate. Why haven't the things in the air tried to kill me? Or the other Angels from Heaven, why has nothing moved, why haven't I moved yet?

What is going on? We have been sent here to bring an end, to all that is, all that has, and all that will be, for Evermore. Why haven't I struck the thing before me, why haven't my wings moved? My wings are what make me an Angel, an Angel from God. God's power is in my wings, they are indestructible. God's power is, was, and always will be. I can't be here floating effortlessly, over the Earth, with all the Angels, without God's power! What is going on? I can't feel my hair drifting, I can't feel my sword, or the power of the portal holding the saltwater. I can't feel my beautiful body; I've looked upon myself so many times, standing nude before a mirror. The love of God all about me, my beautiful body so strong and graceful in the bright sunshine. Long blonde hair, blue diamond eyes, skin like milk, and the taste of me is the same as the best honey made in a honeycomb. Made of milk and honey, protected by God's armor and given God's own power in the form, of wings. This is what is needed to create an Angel of God. With the wings I can fly through a portal to earth. I can fly through a portal to Hell; I was built to come into contact with, and survive any insult, thrown at me by a Demon, Fury, Hellhound, and survive any attack by a Hell's Angel. But I know I can be killed, many of us have been. The lights in heaven are there to remind me of just how many of us have tried to defeat Hell's rage. I always wondered if I would join them in Heaven and shine a light in the night. No matter how seemingly insignificant that light may be. When I fly straight through Heaven, I can be as a wind that touches each leaf on a tree. I can be as the light from the Sun on a flower, or I can be as the sound of bells, ringing in the distance. The ones in Heaven see me, and are moved to tears of joy, and shameless abandon. They begin to dance and sing. It's as if life has just begun, and the first promise God made is: *A brand-new day*.

I fly effortlessly through Heaven and pass gracefully through a portal over Earth, anytime, anywhere. I fly with a protector Angel always at my side, I love life, I love Heaven, I love all the people of Earth, and their souls. I love Angels.

Things made by God are not visible by mortals, they cannot see Heaven, and they cannot see Hell. They can only catch a glimpse of spirits, and sometimes they can see an Angel, be touched by one. Sometimes they can talk to us, and us to them. Always mortals have an Angel by their side until death. That is God's second *promise*. Amazingly, it has happened that an Angel feels so strongly for a mortal, that it gives up its existence in the moment before the mortal will die and may even die in the arms of a mortal. Angels from God are instructed not to be so foolish, as the one thing God has warned is if, when the Angel dies, and before God can recover the power in the wings, the wings may be stolen by a mortal, or worse by a Demon, or a Hell's Angel! I am an Angel from Heaven, I am the most powerful thing God has ever, and ever will be. I am more powerful than even the Fixer Angel from Hell. The weakness I have is, my body cannot handle moving between Heaven, Earth and Hell, therefore, I must pass through a bubble in a portal I can create anytime, anywhere, with just a flash from my wings. This portal opening and closing pulls at the atmosphere, giving warning of my arrival to any messenger from Hell. Thus, I have no chance of a surprise attack and can be attacked without notice once stepping out. I must fully have trust in God's Armor, every time I travel. God has put all his trust in every Angel he creates. God gave me a sword made of lightning, which can cut out the guts of a Demon or Fury. The sword can cut through the toughest hide of a Hell's Angel and can even cut off arms, legs, or even better, cut off its wings. So, I can watch it fall back into Hell, whence it came. God gave me a shield. The shield itself is a portal designed to hold a whole Sea of saltwater. So powerful the shield is, any strike possible by a Hell's Angel is useless to harm the shield, or myself, shielded by the blow. God's promise is to protect me with his love, protect me with the ability to move through the air as wind or a breeze; as well as create a stairway to Heaven for souls to tread upon, to be received at the Gates of Heaven. That's why my hair is golden. Made of the very gold from the streets of heaven to tread upon. Because of God's promise, because of God's will, because of God's protection, because of God's trust. I will promise to protect and trust every soul ever created. This statement is what every Angel from Heaven must state before God, when created, because it contains the four truths: Will, Promise, Trust and Protection. God wasn't fooling around when he designed angels. Angels are God's only hope for the souls on Earth to get to Heaven and not fall to Hell. Where they can be turned into Demons, and Hell's Angels. Where the balance between Heaven and Hell becomes Hell bound, and out of control. If this happens, God will move Heaven closer to Earth. God will become *enraged* at all those in Hell, and God will throw every Angel he can and will ever make, straight at the Heart of Hell. Trying to kill Hell itself and losing his only hope for love, peace, trust, and truth, to destroy Hell, and everything along with it.

I look to my right, then left; there are fourteen of us, Heaven's beautiful Angels: seven of us and seven protector Angels. We had traced the Fixer Angel to this location, I have a shrewd, sagacious plan worked out previously with the other six. We will make an attack here, when the Fixer Angel portals: four of us will be waiting in Hell for him when he slips, that leaves five, plus five protector Angels. If we can divide his team, he will lose, or we will die trying. Too much damage is being wrought here in the desert areas. The thing is, lately the Fixer has had a spree of kills. We have been told to be on guard for some unbeknownst power the Fixer may be using, as the kills were without much contention. If such a skill is assumed by the Fixer, God can equal it. But however, God needs to know the root of the power being used. We have been sent to find the root of it, kill the Fixer, or die trying. Will, Promise, Trust and Protection.

The smoke and stream remain, but a flash, the Fixer and follower disappear. Two of us move to where he was last, two of us move to the location of the follower, three of us go to Hell, this requires a portal. The fixer will be alerted to the arrival. So now we use our well laid-out plan. Those four will not step out of bubble but return here. The 3 of us left here will then portal through and step out 2 minutes later. The fixer should be attempting to use his new power on Angels that don't appear. Thus, we may witness this power and use our surprise entrance to watch and engage them, while not being subject to their plan. The atmosphere stretches, then pulls, the four are gone, we wait. I can still sense the presence of the Fixer, the slight taste of the smoke still in the air. Now it's time, we three plus protecters, now flash our wings, the atmosphere gives away, we each step through the bubble, we are through. HELL! This place is alive with hate. Without God's armor we would be dead instantly. I look unbelievably at the scene before me. Four of God's Angels hang in space before us, **_Here in Hell_**, not moving. They didn't make good of their retreat. We all *now* hang here not moving, all 10 of us! What is going on?! This must be what has happened but wait! The Fixer and his follower Angels aren't moving either! They are fixed on the other four and not us. It strikes me that all eight of them are frozen somehow, like us, but they don't know we are here! God! God, do you see this? Hell can see us, Hell is alive. Creatures of all manner, that aimlessly drift in Hell are moving beneath us. Funny, they don't seem to know of our arrival. One of us must make it back to Heaven. No matter what and bring the information of this power to God. What power can freeze eight of the most powerful things God has ever created, what power can freeze the Fixer Angel, and hold us all above Hell?!!! Concealing us in a cloak, so that Hell itself cannot feel our presence. Hell is alive, Hell is like an egg, it has definite borders that encase it. This protects it from Man and his intentions of power. God encased it so it would **_Rot_**, but instead it thrives. It thrives because of its ability to absorb more souls from Man. The souls here are called lost because they are stripped of God's essence. This powerful elixir is then used to feed Hell and provide what is required to produce all the Demons, Furies, Hellhounds, and Angels of Hell. These are all really things that don't exactly exist; they are all just virtual realities. Hell has a mental aggregate that exists in Hell only. Consuming souls for power and existence, the powerful elixir produced by the essence can be saved up like memories in the brain, then be used to produce the most horrible and powerful Arch Angel, or Hell's Angel.

08/05/16 23:00

The Arch Angel contains the very essence itself, and the hallucinogenic properties therein; to be able to completely and utterly defeat an Angel from Heaven in combat. To understand the Hell's Angel completely, one must become a Hell's Angel. Which is not impossible. Just a little foolish to believe, that one day you might escape Hell, God, and the deliverance of Hell. Or the acquisition of God's power from the essence. To become once again, in mortal condition, and then analyze the Arch Angel and its qualities. However, it could be done, and for now let us consider only that it may have happened and not dwell upon it. For an understanding will become illuminated as the events unfolding now will enlighten and illustrate. The Arch Angel is of God in 'essence' only, but a product of the mind of Hell; therefore, has only a virtual existence. The Angel of Heaven is a creation of God in the form of the indestructible wings, the golden strands from the very streets of Heaven, (this is how souls may climb the stairway to Heaven), the lightning bolt sword, the portal of seawater (shield), and the blue diamond eyes. The blue diamond eyes pierce the mental shield of man, beast, demon of Hell, or and through any reasonable obstacle that confronts the Angel. The blue diamond has the quality of the weapon copper, which protects the Angel from Hellfire, portal through Hell, or into Heaven. Also giving an extreme quality of acuity, not found in any other gemstone.

Being immersed in Hell is unbelievable, the stench of rotting corpses, both human and animal. Extremes of humidity and aridness. Unending suffering, screams, howling, growling. The sound of chains dragging, breaking bones, and huge explosions. The acrid smell of burning flesh, plastic, rubber, wood, petrol, and any number of hallucinogens, the last of which is important because without the hallucinogenic effect on the very mind of Hell, Hell could not envision and establish control of the virtual quality of the immensely powerful **_Hell's Angel_**. And, most importantly, the one and only Fixer Angel. The Fixer Angel is such a complicated, ambiguous, equivocal virtual being, that only one may exist in universe at any one time. This Fixer Angel is Hell's antidote to God's control over Hell itself. The Fixer Angel must be considered in two ways and is always trying to control two emotions of opposite, and equally disturbing, outcomes at once. Hence, its ability to fight on two fronts at once and hinder 4 times the power thrown at it. And now the thing has figured a way to control time and dimensional space in a fixed frame, within its vision. If the area is large, the Fixer spreads this range by using the other Hell's Angels virtual interaction with Hell to spread the effect as far as the Fixer can in time and space, in order to gain an advantage over any combatant he views as a threat. This is the very effect it used to gain leave from its cell in Hell. When first envisioned by Hell to gain control over the coming Christ of God. Both went terribly wrong, and the Fixer Angel is the result of a wrong, never to be foretold by God or Hell. Because of the very equivocal nature of the Fixer and Christ. In both cases we are considering a completely emphatic messiah. Capable of saving Heaven, Hell, or the Earth in two completely different directions of discovery while, maintaining authority of being.

09/05/16 22:30

Now we look at how the Fixer escaped from his cell, while in unbreakable chains, set upon him by God **_and_** Hell itself. The Fixer realized that there was a moment just after the heavy door to his cell pushed open, that it was actually a portal. Every time the master opened the door and tossed in two subjects, the Fixer began studying how he could take advantage of both the master and the portal. He realized that by freezing time just as the master gave him that dejected look, ***that! was the time***. The Fixer used this unique ability to reconstruct the woman's heart, once he ripped it out of her. The master, Hell, nor God knew of the Fixer's ability to freeze time and dimensional space. What an unerudite condition for Hell or God to be in. For the very existence of knowledge is broken down into two senses, being *able*, and to *know*. With the Fixer locked up for eternity, God and Hell thought one of them would be first to figure out, why men idolize women, and hate themselves, for *the* wanting to kill their own souls. When the woman wants to control the man's behavior, and sense of oneness with the world around him. If the Fixer could fix this mistake in the heart of an experienced woman, the master thought he would be the first to calculate an antidote to a possible Christ being by God. God felt that when he sent the Phoenix to rescue the woman at the barred window, the woman would return to the Earth and, with a fixed heart she would spread a sense of uncontrollable decision making among other women, thus stopping man from wanting to kill his own soul and starving Hell of souls ending the Fixer and the need for Christ.

The Fixer Angel, looks, feels, smells, and tastes like everything in Hell. When he looks upon his master for the last time, he flashes his wings. Time and space in the immediate area freeze. The master of the portal is a mere demon, and a far inferior being to the Fixer. The demon is forced to stare at the Fixer. The demon cannot control his hatred of himself in the glare of the Fixer. Once it is of undeniable certainty the demon is going to give up its existence due to the hatred inflicted by the Angel, the Fixer Angel flashes his wings, the demon steps forward towards the Angel in utter anguish and the Fixer Angel reaches out, and with a gesture cuts the demon in two. Takes his control of the portal and pulls it toward himself. The chains are immediately dissolved by the power of the portal. The Fixer enters the portal a free Hell's Angel. Thus, becoming the absolute reason Hell has no power over or, to control the virtual essence in the Fixer. A Hell's Angel with two consciences and each with the ability to conceive alterable outcomes in any instance. Literally a Hell's Angel times eight. This is how the infinity symbol came to be recognized as a sideways *8*. Once freed, He became infinitely endowed with the elixir ***of*** Hell.

I watch intently the scene as four of God's Angels are frozen before four Hells' Angels. The scene is intoxicating and poisonous at the same time. Then without warning, horribly, I see God's Angels losing their armor, as if shedding skin. All four die in an instant. Their bodies disappear in a faint wisp of smoke. Their wings flash and disappear. We flash and portal back to where we were before entering Hell, hoping to regroup, and message Heaven. Our hopes are dashed when stepping out of our bubble. We find ourselves confronted by the Fixer himself. This time there is no freezing, as he flies at us with an intuition in his head that we four are actually helpless to fight once shaken by the deaths of the four in Hell only moments ago. I drop straight to the Earth beneath us. The other three are immediately torn to shreds by the powerful blows from the Fixer and accompanying Angels. Lightning streaks out across the skies, and saltwater falls as like rain everywhere. Lightening is not possible in Hell, and water cannot form there either. These things are only possible here in Earth. The Hell's Angels are pursuing me but instantly two of them are overcome by the saltwater, they flash and disappear in order to save themselves. I fly straight at the other two using ***God's Tears*** to cover me in Brilliance. I am not afraid of these things; they can die too!!! The Fixer's protector is reached first. On a first pass my sword takes one of his wings and half an arm off. It's back to the Fires of Hell for him. Now before I commit to the final battle I flash. Emerging into Heaven, I step fourth from the bubble. No, it can't be! The Fixer is here! In front of me, in Heaven too! I am frozen, he is frozen, most of Heaven closet to us is frozen. I see his hate, I see his pain, I see his split personality. I am utterly ashamed by his empathy. As his consciousness enters my imagination, I lose control of my hold on reality. At once the armor on my body falls off, like shedding skin. I hang nude before this monster, I am ashamed and helpless. Surely, I will die now. He flashes and disappears. I'm in Heaven. I feel like Hell.

10/05/16 22:00

I drift slowly down on to a street. In Heaven the golden streets are soft to touch, flowers grow beside the streets along with shrubs and fruit bearing trees. Butterflies and birds constantly amass in groups and playfully fly by. The sunlight here is splendid and feels warm on the soul. There are no true bells that ring, only the sound of bells ringing in the distance, to announce the passing or passage of Angels. Small sparks pass by illuminating the playfulness of animals in all forms, as they jump and chase the sparks. God has planned all things in Heaven to be as natural and peaceful as a summer rain while the sun still shines. Creating rainbows everywhere, shimmering ponds, and creeks. Fish and all manner of marine life of every kind abound in these waters. Everything feels so smooth that there is even a calmness when the wind blows, causing a kicking up of leaves and dust. Still, it feels as though the most placid pristine water you have ever seen, is laying everywhere. Sometimes you can see clouds billowing up and then they part exposing Heaven's beautiful dark sky and shimmering stars in the distance along with the passing of a Lunar body, shooting stars and comets. Light exists everywhere. Children run and play here and there; men and women walk amongst the children and there seems to be a careless abandon amongst all. Souls in Heaven can appear and fade at any moment. No one here has any sense of time. Time does not exist in Heaven; time stops at Heaven's gate. Time is man's creation, Heaven nor Hell can exist if there is time, or _**Ebb n' Flow**_.

Now I am standing on a street in Heaven. God's pure armor is lying all around me on the street. My beautiful body is standing nude for the first time in a place of absolute pristine elegance and grace. I am made of milk and honey; my feet wear a thin slipper of the finest sheep skin; my hands are dressed in a white silk glove. My fine golden hair streams by my side like the beautiful mane on a fine racehorse. My _**Blue Diamond**_ eyes do not ever tear, Angels need never cry because God's Will, Protection, Trust and Promise, can never allow an Angel to feel fear, and cry as a result. _Tears_ are streaming down my face!!! They burn my skin. My Blue Diamond eyes that cannot cry are crying! I cannot stop the tears from flowing down my face. I am still holding my sword and shield, my wings are still and somehow feeling lost. I feel pain, and I am ashamed of the destruction of God's armor. God will be in front of me at any moment. I am so scared. My mind is racing, and I can't focus on Heaven, all I feel is the Hell that has found its way into my mind. I have been told of the _Elixer of Hell_, how this drug is a derivative of the souls captured in Hell. A _hallucinogen_ exists in the mind of the Fixer at all times, allowing him to cast a perception into the conscience of another Angel of Hell, or Heaven, thus creating the ability of a multi layered attack in synchronized succession without being delayed by communication. Or in the mind of a Heaven's Angel, the perception of perplexing anguish. Imagine _**Hell**_ in the mind of a _**Heaven's Angel**_!!!

Can I tolerate anything more? Can I feel the breeze on my skin or hear bells ringing in the distance? I cannot focus; Heaven is disappearing before my vision. I believe I will die and return God his power, I will drop my sword and shield and give up this ***Ghost of Hell***, A Ghost of Hell in Heaven. I wake up at once! I stop crying immediately. God's armor rises up from the street and dances around me. I feel a presence of Holiness all around! God's armor once again returns to me I am saved, I alone know why. I flash my wings; I step into the bubble, and portal into Hell! This time there is no pulling at the atmosphere no warning of my arrival will be given to any messenger of Hell. The Fixer will not know I am here at all. For the first time an Angel from Heaven, is going to get some Fuck'n revenge on this place! I will fuck up some of this place, get some answers or die trying! As I gracefully pass over the ***River Styx*** and watch the *lost souls* cross over; I notice souls are frantic and gesturing in my direction. I spin and dive straight down. I throw down my shield onto acrid water of the STYX then landing on the shield, I surf the river: my wings are sails pushing me with ease. I force huge plumes of smoke from the river up over the banks the river. This acrid liquid can only exist in the canal made for it; no water can exist anywhere else in Hell, no matter how virulent. Thus, as the STYX rises in the atmosphere of Hell, it immediately becomes smoke and ash, spilling onto the banks of the canal. What wondrousness in Hell!

I am playing in the River STYX. I am the ***MAKO***, flying amongst the lost souls in Hell. The answers are lying at the bottom of this terrible *canal of torture and suffering*. I will spill all its blood onto the banks and expose the truth of the River STYX to the lost souls. Isn't that why they cross over to remain lost in Hell? While they are stripped of the essence of God in their crossing? The Fixer and companion Angel arrive on the other side of the Styx and stare fixedly in my direction. I am pleased by the attention, which I now command. What a wonderful enticing perception to watch. An Angel of Heaven playing in the river Styx, totally unhindered by the lost souls, and exposing the truth of Hell to all those who cross over. Watched by the fixer and his protector. There is a ghost of Hell in my conscience, and it wants revenge. I stop; hang motionless above what was once the STYX, now choked by all the ash built up. While lost souls disappear at an amazing rate. The Fixer is frozen, his protector is frozen. I am not, let's play with you Fixer. I flash and reappear before his eyes, and flash and reappear before his protector. Who now falls in pieces as my sword slices through his entire body with ease. I flash; I'm gone from Hell. I must regroup my thoughts, for I cannot return to Heaven, I don't know how God will accept this reality that exists in me, or if I will eventually be hunted: by *Heaven & Hell*. My allegiance is to Heaven, but I feel like I am at home in Hell. God help me! I know I must **_Surrender_**, for **_Acceptance_**.

12/05/16 22:00

Where in *Hell* is Heaven, where in *Heaven* is Hell? Why should anyone even consider these concepts? Why does the Fixer *freeze* its prey? How does the Fixer control two consciousnesses capable of perceiving two exclusive truths? Why does the Mako fly into Hell to *expose* a truth? Why would I *lie* to tell the truth? Why would I *truthfully* tell you a lie? When the fixer broke his chains and escaped from the *Eternal Test*, he became two personalities to fix the woman's heart; he needed to freeze her life for an instant to preserve the soul. Then he removed her heart and fixed the mistake, sowed it back together, fixed the damage, and used his freeze to restart the heart. However, *saving the soul* is not supposed to be done in Hell. That is why the fixer is so exhausted and weak afterwards. Hate-love, strong- weak, hard- soft, hot-cold, wet-dry, Heaven and Hell. Humm, that just leaves the Heavens and Earth. Go to Hell or come to Heaven.

A long time ago when there was no way to settle a dispute except by fire, people were less likely to lie about the truth. Today good people are making deals with anyone in order to get what they want. Man's power is eroding the Protector Angel's power to steer him on to the path of righteousness. So many people are condemning the other, that many people are becoming lost to the world, and know only hate before they die for: any reason. Then they fall into Hell & add their soul to Hell's Feeding *Trough*. Funny how that's a little like the shape of the river STYX. A river where no such thing can exist. Where is the truth in the Hell? Poisonous water running through Hell strips the soul of its essences and the hides the truth of Hell's thirst for salvation.

15/05/16 22:30

All at once, a protector angel from Hell arrives beside the Fixer. Then another protector angel from Hell arrives beside the Angel from Heaven, with the ghost from Hell in her. Then six more of Hell's angels and their accompanying protectors arrive. Just to the left and higher a massive Bubble in the atmosphere begins to stretch the atmosphere. Heaven's angels are coming. Immediately the Fixer freezes all the Hell's Angels so they cannot surprise attack Heaven's army. Then the bubble opens. Angels, too many to count start to step forth, as they step out and assume positions, they become frozen as well. Once the number of Heaven's Angels stop emerging, the bubble Immediately snaps shut. What a scene! There must be over one hundred of these beautiful angels. Then comes the moment I was waiting for. I am the Fixer, but now I am a protector angel as well. Will she recognize this, or will I die and start a war no one can win? The angel on my right, now the only angel that is not frozen, steps forward. Graceful in every move she starts to dance, everyone can hear bells ringing. A light rain starts to fall. These are not God's tears; this is like a mist and a light rain. Light seems to come from everywhere. Steam and light puffs of smoke drift off every Hell's Angel. And now I see steam and small puffs of smoke from the Heaven's Angel as well! She moves towards Heaven's army. I unfreeze four immediately in front of her. They move to her side, they begin to dance, bells sound everywhere, so unbelievably beautiful.

I send instructions to all Hell's Angels if they move after I unfreeze, I will kill them all myself before I die, here and now. I unfreeze all Angels at once. Immediately the Heaven's Angels part into two groups. The largest group maybe sixty of the estimated One Hundred, group up with the 5 that are dancing and ringing bells. The rest just Hang in mid air not moving. Then I move to my Angel's side and take a position to her left again. She stops dancing and looks at me I can't believe it she is crying. She throws her sword up and the lightning bolt streaks across the sky. Then she tosses her shield, the portal collapses & saltwater rains down on everyone. The Hell's Angels have been warned not to move or face certain death, so they wail, smoke appears while some flare up and start to burn heavily, soon enough the saltwater rain stops, and they recover. She then sheds her armor, and it continues to dance without her. She begins to walk toward me. She is stunningly beautiful. What is she doing. Heaven can wait; Hell can wait. Heaven's Angels are now circling around us. I can freeze them before they effect an attack, and we can escape but will she escape or will she want to die to release the ghost. This angel from heaven stops within six inches of me. She is looking directly into my eyes crying, and not nervous or trembling at all. Her breasts are just away from me, I feel warmth in my body. I feel a strange pull from her. She reaches out and caresses my head and down my left arm, takes my hand and places it on the middle of her chest! "Help! Help. Help me please," she says to me. "Help me to go to the Heavens and take my place with the other angels. Help me please, I surrender to you! I surrender to you." All of the Angels from Hell and all of the Angels from Heaven start to chant the pledge at the same time. I Will Promise, Trust, and Protect every soul from God. Over and over non stopping, I am silent as I have my left hand held in place, over the *Heart of a gift from God*. Her hand holds my hand indicating she wants me to kill her. I take her hand that is free in my other hand, I place it on my chest and for the first time, I feel her skin as I place her hand on my chest. I can't believe it, **I feel alive**, is this possible? Can it actually be possible? I am Dead. Dead! Fucking Dead, to the Dead! What is this, she surrenders to me, we touch the next thing I know, I am not dead anymore? She states, "Can you return me to Heaven and release the ghost in my head? This war does not need to happen. Fixer, you do not need to die here on Earth now. You need to be there at the battle of *Evermore*, only you can stop that battle. Kill me here before you die, and the great battle loses you!" I hold her hand over my heart. I say, "I can kill you. You can kill me. But don't you realize that when the ghost entered you, I became your protector? I am the **Fixer** and your protector. If I kill you, I kill myself. We both fucking die. Right here, Right Now. I surrender to you just as you surrender to me. You can accept me; I can accept you! Heaven and the Hell can wait!"

The angels all around us are chanting the creed. They expect me to kill the Gift form God. They expect to see a battle in which She dies, and the Fixer dies soon after. What they don't know is I am not the Dead anymore. Then I noticed that smoke nor steam no longer drift from me. My wings fall off! The Angel in front of me reaches behind her, pulls her wings off and slams them on my back! Holy shit this is not happening. Next thing an angel from Heaven steps forward and pulls her wings off and affixes them on the back of my beautiful crying Angel. That Angel then drifts upward to Heaven to be a light in the night sky. My Heaven's Angel declares, "That was my protector angel! I am now an angel from Hell as are you. However, you are the Fixer, and you are not dead anymore. You need to go to Heaven and save your soul or you cannot exist till the battle of *Evermore*. You shall die and Hell will replace you. Your replacement will kill me and attack Heaven through me, a rebellion will break out. God will throw every Heaven's Angel at the heart of Hell, and everything will be lost. Go save your soul! I *will* follow you; I will *protect* you I will *promise, and* I will *trust* you, I will. You will, *promise, trust* me, and you will *protect* me. We will be saved. God will accept you. You surrendered. I surrendered. We will be accepted." We flash. We appear In Heaven, for once I am able to stand on my feet and feel the street through my soul. Finally, I am saved. She saved me.

17/05/16 23:00

I stand in Heaven, on the Golden streets of Heaven! I am the Fixer a Hell's Angel, I have almost come full circle, my soul is saved but I cannot wear God's armor. I must return to Hell and cast off my beast-like body. Once back in Heaven, I may purify my body and be able to wear the armor of God. I hear bells ringing everywhere, and I feel the sun on my flesh warm and comforting. I see animals and all manner of insects everywhere, along with Rainbows high into the heavens above. My protector angel walks beside me. I cannot know how she feels because she is still a duality with a Ghost of Hell in Heaven. How is this possible that I can't feel her conscience. I have the ability to see straight through any mental defence. God, I'm the one who stripped Her of her armor. I caused her duality. Hell can't hold Her nor can Heaven. God won't even stand before us in Heaven, while I look like Hell, and she carries a ghost of Hell. I *will, promise, trust,* and *protect* every soul from Heaven. I stop and turn to her. I chant the Angel's creed; Bell's ringing stops, and she stands to chant as well. Then Angels from heaven appear all around. They stay silent as we chant. I can't freeze her though I could freeze the others; but not her, so I can't drive that ghost out of her conscience. I can't find a way to fix this! My eyes of black coal don't hold any emotion the vapor leaking from them is my only defense from certain destruction. We surrendered to each other, our dualities are separate, but our future ***is*** a ***combination***.

While I chant, while she chants, I notice tears streaming down her face. I don't know why she is crying. Her duality is blocking my attempt to intuition and perception. Angels of Heaven cannot cry. This angel is crying. I stop chanting as does she. I reach out for her chest I place my right clawed hand on her chest. She drops her sword, places her right hand on my horrible flesh where my heart should be. I look into her eyes. I see her this time, I am horrified! I cannot feel this! I ripped the hearts out of so many women when in chains and never was I able to see their past lives or feel their passion. What in Hell is going on in Heaven. The Ghost of Hell is killing her! When she surrendered to me the ghost began to intrude into her mental aggregate, once there, it began to disassemble her conscience. Now she is dying before me, and I may be powerless to stop it from killing her. I call out to God. "What hath thou done. Thine trap is not the end you seek. The dis-assemblage of this angel is also a spear to thine own existence. Thou shall not change the future of thine own plan without justification before the surrender of both Heaven and Hell."

"Without my double duality the end of everything will, promise trust and protection of every soul is lost to both Heaven and Hell."

"God answer to this, God, I beseech thee. God stand before us. Give us the future you planned now before it's too late… please…"

As I scream to the heavens with my face turned upwards, I feel her collapse to me. I fall to the ground on my knees. A Hell's Angel on his knees begging God for Help. Lighting begins to form around my beautiful angel and protector. I feel this is the moment I cannot bear to live through. I could have been dead still. I would not feel a thing. God please she is dying, save her take me, anything; she is dying. Then I notice the other angels around us have begun to chant. Then I see Hell's Angels flashing here from where we were standing just moments ago, when I thought there would be a battle to the end of us for our coming together. These Hell's Angels are gathered amongst the Heaven's Angels and are chanting as well. I am struck by a bolt of lightning! It passes through my body and penetrates into my protector as well! Is God going to kill us both here and now? How will I end this life, it's only just begun.

I feel like Hell again! I feel like killing everything in Heaven. I feel hate again; I am the Fixer again! The lightening bolt is gone. I stagger backwards. Holy Fuck the Heaven's wings on my back are gone! Hell's wings are returned to me. My beautiful Angel stands up, she is beautiful. Skin like milk and honey, eyes of blue Diamond, they're not crying anymore. She speaks to me, "God has restored the Ghost of Hell back to you. You are Dead once again, now you know what it feels like to live and die. You are a Hell's Angel and now you and I are Reborn!"

I take a knee and cast my gaze downward. I speak to the Heaven's Angel before me as she picks up her sword and shield. "I am the Fixer; I surrender to you. You are free from pain now and may strike me dead! Dead to you, Dead to Heaven, the Earth, and its souls. I am dead, so fucking dead that even the lost dead souls in Hell fear my passing. I know not what I have done to earn your respect, but I surrender to you before God and His Angels." The beautiful angel standing before me raises her sword to the heavens before me. She says the creed, "I will, promise, trust and protect all God's souls to the Gates of Heaven. And now to the Gate's of Hell! I once was pure and only made of milk and honey. Now I have been taken by a ghost of hell, I have lived a duality, I have been the *Mako* and attacked the River STYX, in Hell itself. I have been utterly driven insane by the ghost of hell and finally killed by my own God. God only, can Kill his Angel and strip it of a duality then cause the Angel to be reborn. God has returned me my soul! He has given me a choice to accept my current position as Heaven's Angel, or to continue as the *Mako*! I accept that the choice is mine, and I *will promise*, *trust*, and *protect* the Mako and follow you! Fixer, I am forever more your protector. I will follow you to Hell, I will even give you a ***guided tour*** if you want it."

The Heaven's Angel rises up holding the shield in front of her, then lets go of it! The shield drops to the golden street below. The portal is disintegrated by the power of redemption in the soul powered golden street. The very power of the Redeemer, who walks the streets of Heaven, and saves the souls who enter and who walk on the streets of Heaven. No shield may touch the golden streets of Heaven. No salt water may fall from the skies of Heaven. God's tears only fall on Earth from the heavens when God's own Angels die; and God *does not cry* in Heaven. So now the portal is destroyed and out spills the salt water, that is instantly turned into pearls. Out they pour onto the streets and everywhere into Heaven!!! This is the first time ever that a shield portal has collapsed in Heaven. The first-time saltwater quickly turns into an innumerable amount of the most beautiful pearls ever seen. Seeing all of the pearls spilling out into Heaven, God then opened Heaven to the Earth allowing the pearls to spill into all the soft mollusks in the Oceans of Earth. Proclaiming that the power of redemption has created the best beauty hidden in a shell of life beneath the oceans for Man to find and give to each other. Man is to remember that giving a pearl is nothing short of the best beautiful mixture of God's tear and the power of Life itself. God gives them freely to man and the whole world to express beauty and kindness amongst His kind.

As the pearls spill outward, some of them come into contact with me, a Hell's Angel. They immediately explode! Causing shimmering lights and giving off rainbow effects in the air. As fire and electricity of any kind is not possible in Heaven. Just as water or any form of life is not possible in Hell. I drift upwards toward my protector Angel, a new confidence is in my every move, as in Hers. My duality now able to see into her conscience, able to perceive her very essence. She feels my incursion, and without hesitation asks me to instill and establish the Ghost of Hell once again into her mind. That once again the Mako may fly into Hell, be amongst the Dead, fly above the Earth to be amongst the living! The Mako must have the truth and will have the truth, so's it will be known to the Living and the Dead. The Mako must have its truth to be known to the living and the dead. All the while I will remain your protector and reside in Hell, and on Earth with you always till the *Battle of Evermore*. Tears are once again streaming down her beautiful face, as she is feeling my hate, my pain and suffering. I am reluctant to agree to the request as I am sure God will not intervene a second time. We are a combination now, a dual essence inside our own minds. The outcome of our combined existence is ambiguous, equivocal. And will not be under the govern or influence of Heaven or Hell. This paradox may lead to the demise of us all, even before I am able To carry out the request. I am the Fixer! I am able to change the outcome of even this. I *will, promise, trust*, and *protect* you, come now my protector.

Pearls are flowing everywhere; rainbows and lights of all colors are flying everywhere. The sight of a beautiful angel of heaven flying above the streets of Heaven with an Angel of Hell at her side is all at once a perplexity, and an embodiment of the combination of a double duality out of the reach of God and Hell. God touches an Angel of Heaven, that angel moves to the side of the Mako, and chants the oath to her, becoming her protector. God touches another Angel; she flies to the side of the first protector, and chants to that Angel. Now the Mako are a trinity. The Fixer Howls so loud that the pearls all around him shake and vibrate. Two Hell's Angels fly to His side. He immediately hits them both a blow that should have killed them but then freezes them striking them on fire. However, they are in heaven and Hellfire is not allowed to be lit here. So, a blue vapor pours off of them and their wounds heal quickly before they expire. Then the fixer howls again, and flies around the group like a wild Fury. He repeats the oath, "I will promise trust and protect All Souls of God to heaven and Hell. Come now Mako we have to finish this, come now Mako, follow me to the gates of Hell and bring your protectors with you. I will give you all a guided tour. Hell won't be your home but to truly be the Mako you must return to the river Styx and receive the truth you seek. You must receive the Ghost of Hell into your conscience once more and you must commit to your **Child of Truth.**"

All of the Angels begin to fly in dizzying circles in every direction around the Mako and the Fixer, then flashes from their wings as the Hell's Angel's, two at a time disappear. In a synchronized movement with a *Flash*, the trinity, the Fixer, and his accompaniment all disappear together. Heaven, now partially covered in pearls, once again looks, and feels like Heaven. The sounds of the bells ringing in the distance, calm water on the ponds, rainbows shimmer in places. The sounds of the laughter and animals move about the countryside. Birds fly as do butterflies and little sparks of light. But there are three figures walking down one of the golden streets. One of the figures is *Transparent*, one is *Diaphanous*, and as the *Third* one walks upon the golden street, with each step taken, water splashes even though no water is evident on the street. Heaven is a vastly different place it seems now that the Fixer has been reborn here. It also seems that there will be much to answer for soon. The Mako will be back to search for the hidden truths that lay here too! These three must now decide the outcome of the discovery and the outcome of the demise of the Mako, should the truth become aware to Hell itself. The Holy trinity must walk the streets of heaven and lay down the *way* to the truth, then they must return to Hell and strike a covenant with Hell, that the demise of the Mako will not prevent the Fixer from fulfilling his position on the front line of the battle with the Angels of Babylon. Man must not find Heaven and must not find Hell. Hell must not expose itself to Man.

23/05/16 22:30

So, in the beginning the Trinity is in play. Man has spread out across Asia, Europe, Africa, and throughout the Americas. Different religions have been set out, and some of the originals have splintered. God moved Heaven far away from Earth so Man's power could not find it. Hell has always been sealed in an egg created by God to keep it from spreading its *Hate* and ebullience throughout the Universe. In the beginning God, had buried truths in Hell, on Earth and in Heaven. They are the constant that keeps everything in flux. Keeps everything fluid and maintains the constant push and pull of the cosmos. Man is moving out of the early days of the first metal forgeries. Powerful kingdoms are springing up everywhere on Earth. Early Governments have little chance of holding on to power through as the *God-Head* leaders of the time can't control land Barrons and their army's take of pillage, plunder and the slave-trades. Man will eventually strike a Civilization Agreement with Land Barrons. Thus, a way for Godheads to control vast wealth and huge kingdoms. Hell, constantly sends messengers to Earth in an attempt to pull any soul off the path of righteousness. Thus, through the early deaths of Angels by luring anyone to riches instead of existing in peace. Kill a Protector Angel at the right time and a whole segment of people can suffer for hundreds of years, due to the loss of governmental control and its protection. Which more often than not leads to slavery and certain damnation of a vast numbers of souls. The plans are now in place for the coming storm! Man, Science, Medicine, the word of Law, and Bureaucracy.

Heaven, Hell, and time. What do these things have in common? Well, Heaven does have stars moving in certain regular synchronized movements, which means a timing as such has been applied to the environment of Heaven. Hell has an encasement surrounding it completely. However, as souls are amassed in the Bowels of The River STYX, and thus the whole mass of Hell pulses with life. This also suggests a rhythmic tide. Time, the breakdown is: A tide with a different termination, or ending, side of, and extreme point. Now we know that time ends at the gate of Hell, also at the gate of Heaven. But now we know that timing is required to keep both heaven and hell with spirit. Spirit, this is how the truths are buried, the spirit in Hell yearns for salvation. The truth is buried under the River STYX, and this is how the stripper takes the holy power from the soul to feed Hell. Thus, the soul is lost in Hell and lost to Heaven, once stripped of its essence. The truth buried in Heaven is under the golden streets. This is the first place the soul comes into contact with Heaven as with the first step. The truth is in the meaning of Gold itself. Ductile, malleable metal. The last is Guild, where *All* belong to the same class. The soul is drawn to the gold and stepping on to the streets becomes shaped into the heavenly body that perfectly matches all others. This *Is* the promise of redemption. The Gold of Heaven pays for all sins. The redeemer pays for all sins spiritually. The holy spirit continually replenishes, the gold for the redeemer as he walks on the streets and the Holy water splashes from his feet to cleanse all souls.

The souls in Heaven are saved, the souls in Hell are stripped. The souls on earth are made at the time of conception. God then assigns an angel and its protector to the new soul. The newborn baby either dies too early or lives a full life. The soul is either protected, trusted, promised to Heaven or Hell, by an accompanying Heaven's Angel or Hell's Angel. The truth buried on earth is to 'conceive' itself. *All* is in this truth. To conceive is to have something from nothing. Hence the statement nothing *is* worth the cost. To *conceive* is to construct a soul, a soul comes from the *nothing* to become *everything* that was, that is, and that will be. The fact that the angels fly to and from Heaven or Hell and pass over the Earth has no effect on the time, nor does the effect of time on Earth affect the passing of Angels. Hell sends Hellhounds and demons to Earth to scare souls and people into making rash decisions. Heaven's Angels intercept these ill-fated grievances easily, their armor alone will destroy a Hellhound, Fury, or Demon. Hell needs souls and can't always afford to send Hell's Angels to do battle, so distractions are needed. Heaven's Angels can fight as two always but lack a duality. The Christ has a duality but was not intended to fight, only absorb the sin of man. The Fixer was designed to use his duality to mislead the redeemer thus limit the usefulness of Christ's duality. As Mankind becomes more powerful His arrogance and greed strips the power of the redeemer: Christ. Heaven's Angels lose the ability to protect man and his soul as then the soul is easily misled.

24/05/16 22:30

Now we find man in the earlier days before recorded history. Metal forging is in its infancy, and water transport is limited to rivers, lakes, and the Mediterranean Sea. Travel to and from the island of Japan out into the Indian Ocean. As well as travel back and forth across the Bering Strait, Black sea, & Red sea. Already at this time information gathering and trade routes are being established across the Atlantic Ocean by barges. The Atlantic trade route will grow to be extraordinarily strong soon, as the main political force is African woman who control Africa as a whole, from the eastern side of the continent. Later they would be called the Amazonian Kingdom. Travel by water across the smaller oceans is dangerous but the tonnage and the travel is safe enough to establish a trade route. However, barges sent out on the tumultuous journey across the Atlantic is not fruitful. Barges in great numbers are lost to storms and get lost in the great many changing currents. Some do get through, fewer still get back to the northwest of the African coast. Barges are set adrift from the Southern coast to be carried by the currents to the North coast of South America. The Barges are launched from the Central American area to hopefully be landed near what is to become Morocco. Many people who get across to the Americas stay and build up large colonies. Later as wealth builds both in the Americas and in Northeastern Africa, trade routes become strong as being able to some what control the barges with steers and early sails become useful as sea captains start to chart the stars enroute. This is the beginning of the cocaine, opium, White & Red Thin line.

The Thin Red line, The Thin White line. Much later when Man has gained control of the study into molecular composition and having the ability to study cellular structure of any biological specimen with the use of an Electron microscope. He will find the evidence of cocaine in wide use in areas of Africa and the old Babylonian Empire. As well the use of opium and hashish, in areas of South America and the Central Americas. Drugs have always been Man's best way of imagining possible spiritual routes to any God or Demon. Some people gained an ability to control drug use to the point where reason became real outcomes. The Soothsayer was born. Contact with the Angels were now possible; however, not believable by the masses. And predictions fell short because of unforeseeable events, leading to the *death* of the Soothsayer. This is the time of many conquests via armies in the Northern areas of Europe and Asia. The African, and Babylonian Empires are extremely powerful. Mongolia and the Tibetan Shamanism are very much in control on the eastern side of the Himalayas. It is during this time that the Fixer and the Mako will come to Earth looking for truths buried by God as to the very nature of soul building. Early in prehistory man has not made the sound board, a particularly important discovery, to understand the way sound transposes over and through the use of a harp. Thought to be the most beautiful sounding string instrument, it was offered to Angels in the early gilded cage. Man could not understand that sound needs to "bounce" to frame resonating waves. Which is what is happening when you listen to yourself telling a story to someone.

In Heaven as in Hell, time is nonexistent. Angels move back and forth between realms with no concern for Life or the Tides. Seasons on Earth are colorful changes in the perceptions of the mind. Passing like beautiful panoramas through the *Lenses of the Senses*. Souls from the future may be in Heaven at the same time as souls from the past. Souls in Heaven are not bound by time or the *current* that produces Time, Tides, or the movement of the Universe. The same is true of Hell. Souls are lost at an amazing rate at different times on Earth. But Hell has no interest in a "when" you arrive to The River STYX. The only interest Hell has in a soul is its arrival, and that the essence is given off in its passing through it. The Mako flew into Hell, avoided the Fixers freeze because of the ghost of Hell in her head. She then surfed the STYX causing it to rise up and become ash on the banks of which choked off the flow of the river. But the Mako did not find the truth beneath the flow. Hell used its Angels to remove the ash, and the poisons river once again began to flow in its channel. Stripping the souls that cross over. Hell felt no pain and essentially lost no time due to the inconvenience made by the Mako. So now, once again the Mako and the Fixer make an appearance in Hell with a large number of Angels! The entire crew shows up unannounced because of the Fixer's control of Hell's atmosphere. The reason is all the Heaven's Angels and accompaniment's Entourage. The Heaven's Angels may have been attacked when stepping out of their bubble by Hell. Hell has made no covenant with any Heaven's Angel ever. The Fixer will have his work cut out for him.

Hell has but one truth buried at the bottom of the STYX. Hell does not want any lost soul to find it nor any Hell's Angel. The possibility of a Mako here in the Hell is an unwanted occurrence, and the Fixer will have to prepare for battle on a new and more scary scale before any such covenant is struck. Hell's Angels are flashing into the Hell two at a time from the formation in Heaven. The Fixer and his protector arrive with the others. Angels are not affected by place or time. They can move in and out of Hell or to Earth during any age on Earth and back to Hell or Heaven like no time has passed in their respective homes. Time goes by on earth because of Man's free will. Time stops at the Gates of Hell or Heaven. The Fixer uses his duality to connect with the other Hell's Angels and freezes all Hell!!! The Heaven's Angels step out from their bubble to find Hell frozen, and immediately, so are they. The soon to be again Mako steps out directly in front of the Fixer just as planned. The Fixer looks into the eyes of his new protector. She looks into the eyes of the Hell itself. She feels the hate, and the pain the lost souls of Hell. She would be overwhelmed but for her wanting to be the Mako once more, and then for the second time her armor falls off! Again, she stands nude before the Fixer and all Hell itself!!! This time it will be different. This time there will be no going back to Heaven as a Heaven's Angel ever again. This time she will become the Mako forever and forever more the Mako will fly in the eyes of all Mankind.

26/05/16 18:00

All Hell is frozen! Time is nonexistent, but for the *Freeze* by the Fixer Her body cannot be burnt by Hellfire while her armor is off. The Fixer transplants the Ghost of Hell into her conscience, it takes hold, and she is free again! Her God's armor rises up and once again is clad upon her body. This time the Holy Water droplets are gone; the armor is now blackened by the *Hate* in *Hellfire*. The lustrous shine is beautiful, to see it, truly is transcendence in fluid motion. God now reaches across the expenses, touches the Mako, her wings disappear they are replaced with wings from Hell. Tears stream down her face from her eyes, she is not Heaven's Angel anymore. She is not a Hell's angel either. She truly is the Mako, she flys around Hell while it is frozen. Hell is furious with the Fixer and the Mako, but it is powerless to stop them. When Hell freezes over the Mako will fly to the STYX and discover its truth. The truth will set the Fixer free. Hell will fight the outcome of the truth. This will be a dangerous period, for all Hell and Heaven will be included in this fight. Now the Mako once again surfs the STYX on her shield while holding her golden sword high. The STYX pours up ash on the banks, the sight of which is Incredulous! The Mako is still crying and she can hardly see. Tears of Hate, fear, love, loss, discovery, pain, and joy are blurring her vision. The STYX is disembowelled onto the banks, and the Mako discovers that Hell is actually hiding the truth of salvation beneath the STYX! The Mako then begins to replace the ash into the canal. The Mako intuitively knows her fate.

A tearing at the atmosphere everywhere in Hell. The Fixer is bemused by the occurrence What more Heaven's angels? A War here in Hell?! I can freeze them all!! The Mako will have to make a decision: Kill them all or *Die* instantly when I unfreeze all of them. Wait this is different, what the Fuck?! Here in Hell? They can't come here. Things are fucked for sure; I'll have to unfreeze everyone and hope the confusion screws things up enough to get the Mako through a portal. The atmosphere splits everywhere. Heavens angels step out in an unconceivable number. The *Trinity* has arrived here in Hell! The Transparent one, the Diaphanous one, and the one who **walks** upon water. Except that no water, not even Holy water is possible in Hell as he takes every step an illumination is emitted and an ash drifts from beneath his feet. They continue to walk to the banks of the STYX and stop to look at the ash laden canal and then they stand and stare towards the Mako. Why aren't they frozen? What are they doing here? How can they come here into Hell? They are Holy personages. Here in Hell, can they still be Holy? The Mako flies to the Fixer and stands in his gaze. She looks into his mind and the Ghost of Hell talks to him personally. "Your puzzled mind has the best of you Fixer! What the fuck did you think would happen? The Trinity can't be frozen, nor can you freeze the Mako, *they are all Dualities*, and those three over there: Can tear this place to pieces! Whether you like it or not! Unfreeze everything!! God be with you and the Mako!"

Before the Mako can finish the last statement, the Diaphanous one flashes to be beside the Fixer and looks directly at the Mako. Piercing into the Mako's duality as the Mako backs up slowly. The Mako speaks from the mind of God, "Fixer! You will have to unfreeze everything. You cannot think an outcome of this and try to carry it out by surprise! We the Trinity can also freeze everything. We can also melt down Hell itself if necessary!! We need you to keep your head and your assaults to yourself. We have not come here to challenge you, or your position. We have come here to align the **Truth Child** with Heaven. This child cannot understand the truth's reasoning by simply exposing them one at a time. The truths have been laid down very carefully, and more comprehensively than even a duality can perceive! The **Truth Child** will only spread fear amongst the Angels with the knowledge of the discovery."

"You release the Angels. I will freeze the Hell's Angels only. I will control the Heaven's Angels. I cannot freeze you or the Mako. If you flash with her Hell will hunt you. Heaven will hunt you. I will hunt you down and destroy the Mako before your eyes! You must make good your destiny to be on the front line at the battle of *Evermore*. You will be there, even if we have to replace you with another!" The placidity of him reveals he is God. The Fixer realizes, he has more respect for God than any Deity. He unfreezes Hell! Instantly I can't look onto the light of God. I the Fixer am rendered powerless in Hell. The Transparent one is the Holy Spirit, and of whom disappears into all the Heaven's Angels. All Hell is on fire!!!

26/05/16 18:00

The Hell's Angels are frozen, the Heaven's Angels are held by the Holy Spirit. The Christ is now beside the Fixer. The two of them cannot connect; the Fixer was created to destroy the Christ. The Christ was designed to absorb the sins of man and save the souls so they would not arrive here in Hell. The Mako, herself now a duality, is out of the realm of Heaven and Hell. God is impossible to look upon! The brilliance of light is spread out from a point to everywhere in Hell!! God is moving separately from the light source; God will control Hell, and the Fixer will be saved by the grace of God. The Mako is the only duality that cannot be controlled and must decide to remain the protector of the Fixer or run to the world and bring only pain to Man and ruin to Heaven. As the Mako I only, can know what *has* and *is*. What *will*, is not mine. I am seeking only truth; the Ghost of Hell is how I am able to open Heaven or Hell from inside. Hell can't control the Hellish Ghost while it is in my conscience; God can't control it either, I need the truth to fulfill my destiny; however, the Fixer cannot lust after the truth, knowing God saved him in Heaven.

I am with the Fixer; the truth will wait in Heaven, and on Earth. "Fixer I am with you; I am on your side. Fixer come to me, we will stand together, we will be! Hell cannot allow God to hold sway we must return to Heaven to do Gods bidding and I will be at your side always". Heaven's Angels begin to step into a portal. We flash and are gone to Heaven; God is alone in Hell. God lifts the controlling power! Hell is on fire! God is light!

28/05/16 23:00

Hell speaks: "God, I have a covenant with you; you cannot break it! If you break this covenant Heaven and Hell will start to break down. Your precious Mankind will stop providing souls. You and I will starve; time will leak into our exile and consume us! I am HELL, you cannot break your covenant with me!!"

"I will hunt this Mako, and the Fixer to the death. I plan to replace the Fixer with one that is truly Hellish!"

"I want the Mako, you must deliver the Mako to me. The river STYX will be fixed easy enough, but the Mako has my Ghost of Hell in her. I want it back, and the Mako is to die where this started, on the banks of the Styx. God I am HELL!! Hear me! I will not stop until I have what I want, no matter what the cost is!"

"I am light, I am, I will, I promise, I protect every soul that man makes, Even if I am delivering that soul to Hell. That is the covenant I have with you".

"I am, that is all that is needed to be on your *Seething* breath. I *will*, you can count on that. I *promise*, every promise made by me is fulfilled. I protect even your soul. I *protect* the soul of Hell, and it lives in the STYX!"

"I command thee Hell, I am God your Lord, I command thee Hell, you will not **instruct** your Lord, or I will bring about your **End** by thine own hand! Here and now at whatever the cost!"

"The **Truth Child** is a necessary distraction for the Fixer. More Truths will be discovered. The Fixer will be set free."

"Hell will hunt the Mako I will promise, trust and protect the Mako to the gates of Hell. You will have your revenge, the battle of '**Evermore**' will have its Fixer!!"

Hellfire is the worst thing a soul can imagine. Souls that are backing up in a line before the River Styx are being exposed to a **_Hell_** on fire, as the **Rage** moves about, and back and forth, up and down the STYX. The canal must begin to flow again. Hell speaks: "I will have the essence of God running through me again! I am HELL! I will have my taste of Heaven. I will have my Angels take Hell to the Earth."

"I will take Hell to Heaven, and I will have my revenge on the Mako. I will exact another phantom from the STYX!"

"I will use it to draw out the Mako, and if I can, I will destroy the Fixer and replace it with a *Fucking Angel* that doesn't get to feel anything!!"

"A duality that fucks things up on Earth, and in Heaven is what I'm planning".

"God commands me, I will obey, I will because I am Hell. Go ahead Fixer; knock on Hell's Gate I've been waiting!" The brightest light Hell has ever seen, is beginning to fade as God quits shedding his light and leaves Hell.

God doesn't require a portal. God is light, God is in everything and **_Is_** everywhere at the same time. God moves about the Universe without effort or need for transport. Hell doesn't even **_Truly Understand_** this. God's truth is undeniable in the Universe and needs no coinage. God flashes as light and his spirit moves with grace throughout everything, everywhere, and finally arrives at the *Gates of Heaven* itself. Everything about Heaven is now of a Pearlescence as: when the Mako released the portal of saltwater on the street of Heaven, pearls poured out from the Heavens. What a beautiful sight the Pearl-clad Gates of Heaven, *THE* **_Pearl Nautilus_**.

The Pearl Nautilus, the Gates of Heaven are at the portside of the Pearl Nautilus. This vessel is captained by Nimoü. The Spirit, and Breath of God. God is in everything everywhere, and now in Heaven onboard the Pearl Nautilus. Heaven's Angels in a number too great to count, portal into heaven. They disappear as fast as they emerge into heaven to become as wind gently blowing, or light passing, and the sounds of bells ringing in the distance. The Fixer flashes into Heaven along with the Mako. The Fixer and the Mako make their way down a golden street. The Mako is now not allowed to touch the street just as the Fixer cannot. Souls burn in the head of the Fixer. The Mako has a Ghost of Hell in her Head from the River STYX. Every step they take is just above the street, as smoke drifts from their feet. The street heals itself behind them after thy pass. God has prepared the way they must walk in Heaven. The Mako has a protector angel with her. The Fixer has a Hell's Angel and its protector with him. The way has been set; the path they must take will bring them past and under the Helm of the Nautilus. The group of 6 stop on the street directly below the Helm, this is the '**_Crossroads_**' in Heaven. Now the Trinity walk toward them from 'out of nowhere', from a point just in front of them! To their left and right, souls run, jump and dance. Lights bounce in the air, butterflies and birds dart all around. The Trinity stops, the diaphanous one speaks: "I am your God. I am the one that has breathed life into all souls in Heaven and the ones in Hell. I have brought you to the Cross-Roads in Heaven!"

God, "There is this reason I brought you to the Cross-Roads: I now *charge* the Mako that she discovers the truth buried here! This is how the Fixer will be set free from the discovery the Mako found in Hell. The two combined *truths* will be the freedom the Fixer requires." The Mako rises up slowly while gazing downward, towards the group of five who remain looking at the Trinity. At the crossroads of Heaven, looking to the left is the Starboard, to the right is the Port side, in front of them is the Stern, and behind them is the Bow. The four directions in Heaven are: *Entrance*, *Loyalty*, *Orientation*, and *Mission*. The truth of the crossroads is **Will**. One, who **Enters** here, must be **Loyal**, **Orient**, and conduct their **Mission** here in Heaven. Gods Will, will be done in Heaven. The truth of Salvation in Hell is buried under the STYX, because it is the '*stripper*' of **Souls**. The 'essence' is God's '**Will**' and the true power of God. When you first reach the Crossroads, you must have God's **Will** to go in any direction in Heaven or on Earth. This is the truth of the crossroads anywhere, it is universal; therefore, the Fixer must be set free. I now descend slowly to stand before the Fixer. Mako: "I am speaking to you Fixer, not the Ghost of Hell. I have made the discovery of the Truth buried here beneath the Crossroads. Together with the Truth I discovered in Hell under the STYX; I now release thee from the bondage of Hell! I tell thee that Salvation is what you seek, and here at the crossroads is where you find your '**Will**' to go in any direction in the Universe. Your '**Will**' sets you free Fixer! Salvation is not possible without the Will to take your direction."

The Fixer is motionless, the Christ now walks past us and down in the road behind us. Water splashes up on us as he passes, beads stick to me here and there, and to my Heaven's Angel, where they land on the Fixer and the other Hell's Angels, flashes of light scatter. The Christ walks in the direction of Mission. The Diaphanous one turns right and walks toward Orientation. The Transparent one turns around and walks toward Loyalty. The Transparent one says to the Fixer as he leaves: "Choose wisely, your **direction here**, and your **Will**, will lead you to your Salvation." Then without notice there appears two pairs of wings, floating in midair above the crossroads. The Mako turns to look at them. They are beautiful the Fixer rises above the Crossroads and announces: "I **Will** that I walk with the Holy Spirit, I will follow him." There is a bright flash of light from the Crossroad. The Fixer and Mako are transfixed as their wings fall off and disappear into the Golden Street. The Heavens' wings take their place on their backs. God speaks: "These things that are done at the crossroad cannot be taken back, for now you must walk the road to your destiny. Salvation lies in your loyalty to each other. The Mako is even now, being hunted by Hell. Hell will never stop until it has its revenge!" That is the true **_Hate_** that burns in Hellfire 'Revenge'. God: "Fixer you must be loyal to the Mako if She is to discover the other truths. The Mako must die at the hands of Hell on the Banks of the STYX. Fixer you must avenge the Death of the Mako at the front line of 'Evermore.'"

29/05/16 22:30

Fixer: "I am here! Mako, do you remember my Will? Mako I am here at the front line of Evermore! When first you fought me, I froze you, I put the ghost of Hell in you. Your armor fell off. I left you alone in Heaven, your nude body. So beautiful, made of milk and honey. Mako, I am looking directly at one of your sisters now. She looks a lot like you. She is beautiful, her armor is deadly to me, but she is frozen like you were, soon her armor will fall off like most of all the Heaven's Angels here. God is in everything he is everywhere. The Holy Spirit is here too, Hell is here, because I am here. Below us the Earth is older than we were then. The Earth has changed with the advance of Man. Man fell pray to science and politics. I count 25000 years since the Mako was first confirmed by the Ghost of Hell. How do these people justify their existence?"

They hate each other, they make debts and build Empires. Their offspring then break the bonds that hold the empires together, and war breaks out causing millions to die needlessly. Souls are gathered by Hell's Angels in droves and then driven straight to Hell. Hell has made many gains from the souls of man in the last years. Now Hell feels, *with the Mako taken at the banks of the STYX*; that it surely has the power to break the Trinity. Here now at Evermore, Babylon and its Angels are here. The Mahdi has arrived; the Al-Masih ad-Dajjal is among us. Also, Armilus Eschaton has come with Kalki, Maitrya, The Samael Tannin or Tunannu, and Hybris. The four hoarse men have ridden out across the Earth, and war is everywhere the air is insipid, the ground is barren, the water is poisonous and tainted.

30/05/16 23:00

I hang in the air, motionless, my blackened charred body is grotesque, burnt by the fires of Hell. The look of me is muscular, large powerful chest, a spine that stands out on my back. Legs like that of a powerful horse, but long clawed feet instead of hoofs. My arms are long, powerful heavily boned, ending with clawed hands. My face looks like that of a tiger, completely burnt to the bone, only the armor of burnt flesh is left on the bones of the face. There are no eyelids. The eyes are of blackest coal and have a shine of the Dead. The bluish vapor that pours out all around the eye opening, is the result of the Hell fire on the coal, and the mixture of the souls that burn in my head. The essence leaks out and continuously supplies the vapor. I look, feel, taste, and smell like Hell. On my back are the wings that God gave me thousands of years ago when the Mako stood at my side at the Crossroads in Heaven. The wings don't even look more than minutes old. But they have carried me through so much since first they came to me. I look around without moving. The sky is full of Angels, Heaven's Angels and Hell's Angels; Too numerous to count, too numerous to grasp even as a duality. God and Hell have put everything into this final battle. God has promised to completely destroy Hell by throwing down every star in Heaven, straight at Hell to obliterate it from any place it may hide. Hell has promised to destroy every Heaven's Angel and then attack the Pearl Nautilus with everything it has left. All the grains of sand, in all the beaches of the Earth. We are all just grains of sand. I **will**, *promise* *trust* and *protect*, the *ebb of the tide* has just exposed us at the *End*.

02/06/16 23:30

Hell's Angels flash in to view. Heaven's Angels portal and step from their bubbles. The Fixer and the Mako step out of portals. These are the 6. The Mako must find truths on Earth, and she will start here in the Himalayas that are a part of Southern Asia. The great Mountains are home to one of the future seers *"The Tibetan Empire"*. Buddhist Monks, Spiritual leaders with a special ability to visualize future events, and variations of each event. This is made possible through the use of powerful stimulants, opium, hashish, and now, but rare and only available in limited supply cocaine. Also, with the use of a newly discovered game that we call Chess in the modern world. Called in Aristotle's time Latruncularius. During the great African empire, "*Skaak*" and in area of the Chinese lands, "棋". The game plays on a board of 64 evenly sized squares of opposite colors, a duality. The board is marked with numbers: 1-8 on each side, and letters of the English language: a-h. You will notice the board starts with the number 1 at each end of play. This means that 1 is 8 and 2 is 7, 3 is 6… and so on. One field of play overlaps the other, another duality. The game has 16 pieces or figures on each side in the first two rows of squares. The back rank consists of an Elephant, Spearman, Angel, Soothsayer, Godhead, Angel Spearman, and finally an Elephant. The second row of eight are all trained *Fighting Monks*. These pieces are placed on both sides of the board in order. The right-hand corner of the board must be a white square with the Godhead on its opposite color and the soothsayer on its color (light and dark colored pieces) . The pieces move one player in turn each, and each piece has a specific type of movement. By writing the letters and numerals on the board. A location on the board can become a historical location, and the entire game can then be historical fact, for the use of study. Thus, a way to analyze each outcome and future outcomes, analyzed by the use of setting a time limit on each *game, and player*; of which sees the mortality in each piece, thus giving the game "Life", and the fighting monks become the souls on a game board handled by a player. In a game struck by the *Hands* of time. Trying to find one outcome at a time the forces at play on the board become transcendent, allowing the mind to combine thought and movement, by opposing consciences' in each of the two players. Allowing each player once skilled, to experience a sense of duality. And doing so on a powerful drug; the mind is able to imagine himself as a duality even if only during the time the drug affects the conscience and while struggling against the forces at play.

Now, the Mako is a *Powerful Being* because this is the land of transcendence, and the time is that of transposition. Vast numbers of people are working the land in large, luscious valley areas. Thus, providing huge food quotas that support large armies. For the first time in Man's history, education is being practiced among a large number of wealthy people. Some are removing themselves to isolated places high in the Mountains of the Himalayas. These people begin to practice sensory deprivation. All the while, communing in groups high above in fortress clinging to the Mountain Headlands. Generations go by and record keeping begins. Rudimentary at first, and insight is slow but with the use of trained scribes, history taking begins. Followed by scholarship, sect and secularism. Priesthoods, devotions, meditation, yield long string theory devotees. They produce skilled deliberators, able to follow a particular path of thought on one skill over several generations. Along with the historical material, scholars' of any doctrine, can reasonably conclude out-comes of many personal experiences with good results. Once these theoretical lines of thought are analyzed by scholars of the time, they begin to realize the need for a way to utilize '*dualities*' of reasoning. Along with the use of drug induced sensory deprivation. The most skilled of each sect decide to have contests of physical prowess and mental conditioning. It's at this time the game Chess or *Skaak* is born and leads to the first future-seers better known as *Prophets*.

The group of 6 will move amongst these people of devotion and look for any sign of truths. Hell will hunt them anywhere, and that includes *this place*. I fly over vast expanses of what will be *Xizang Zizhiqu*. These are the days of *Nuwa & Fuxi*, the Mako is with me as well as our 4 protector Angels. The Mako has told us to fly in the direction of Kunlun Mountains. The *Tarim Pendi*, a dry and arid landscape. It's of no matter to us the people here can't see us fly, I dive down to skim the surface of the land as I gaze around, I feel Hell's presence. I smell Hell; I look up to the group. Two of them are drifting smoke, the Hells Angels, the other three don't. I

do; my burnt body still smokes as I fly. I see two more smoke trails behind the group I flash, I briefly pass through Hell, Holy Fuck! I've never seen so many Hell's Angels, and a huge gathering of Hellhounds, demons and furies, I flash. I appear in front of the two trailing the group I freeze them. I want the truth this time. I'm not the Mako; I look into the burning souls of these two *Fucking things*. They know they are about to die for real this time. I get the message loud and clear. I unfreeze them; I wave them to follow, we are on the group in seconds. I Scream and Howl until the group stops. I quickly enlighten them. We are about to be attacked, these two have been sent by God, and not Hell. They will exchange wings with us, so we can better hide during the battle. The smell of Hell is all around us here on Earth, I look down and the ground seems to be moving and alive with Demons.

Two Hell's Angels fly to be beside the Mako and the Fixer. Flashes of light and a large pull on the atmosphere. Bubbles opening, and Portals opening everywhere, the Mako and the Fixer exchange wings with the Hell's Angels. Holy Shit! They are here; the Trinity has come along with more Heaven's Angels, the sky is illuminated by the presence of God, The Holy Spirit and The Christ. There are new streaks of light and smoke coming from the East and the West sides of China. The whole sky is alive with spirits and dragons. There is something different about what is occurring. It appears as though our presence has not gone unnoticed by scouts of the Eurasian Deities. Zeus, Hades, and Poseidon. Indra, Yama, and Varuna Yahweh. The Babylonian Angels, and *that* smell? The smell of hallucinogens, such as opium, hashish, cannabis and poisonous toxins coming from fires burning Fungi on the mountain slopes. There are large Sea serpents swimming up the swollen river. I see a Gargantuan sized turtle and monsters from Hell running along the ground!! Some of them can fly, there are colors drifting in the air; these are gas clouds used to feed the virtual demons, as well as, to strike fear in the hearts of the Angels of God. Man will see these days of war in the Heavens as meteor showers, extreme amounts of rain, and Lightning bolts of *unimaginable* frequency. Volcanoes will erupt, the Earth will shake and split! Upheaval of the Land, and Mountains will crumble. Meteors will strike the Earth, and streak across the sky, fires will erupt burning toxic gasses that escape the Earth. Oceans will wash up all manner of beasts from deep under the sea onto beaches. Huge whales, squid, & sharks. Tornados will literally throw fish all over the land and toss livestock miles away into lakes and oceans. Hurricanes will blow from the ocean to the coastal areas, causing tidal waves to flood vast areas with saltwater. This will change the bays and islets, wipe out cities, fishing, farms and totally annihilate small civilizations; as well as whole species of animals and already stressed vegetation. Whole forests' burn, rivers change course, lakes dry up. Deserts appear where grasslands were, Areas ravaged by floods remain so for decades, mass starvation of animals and humans. These Earthly changes will one day be called "Continental Drift". The sky blackens with birds and insects in their millions. Huge migrations of animals traverse the land trying to escape the floods, fires, and smoke from toxic plumes. This is why it *Smells like Hell* on Earth, howling, burning flesh, poisonous gases, breaking bones, and the screams of suffering people and livestock. The sky is continually changing colors the eerie iridescence makes it extremely hard to tell what time of day it is. Celestial bodies not seen before travel across the daytime sky and illuminating the night sky like it was actually daytime. These planetoids block the sun, causing Solar Eclipses not seen before by Man. All of the Gods have come to pay homage to the Mako, the Mako is named in older languages on Earth, some these are: ابن الله الحقيقي , Kindvandie Waarheid, 真理之子, Anak ng Katotohanan, Đứa con của sự thật, Дитя истины, το αληθινό παιδί του Θεού, 진실의 아들, ਸੱਚ ਦਾ ਬੱਚਾ, सत्य का बच्चा.

The different religious people were terrified by the loss of life, the volcanoes, flowing lava, the fire storms, streaks of light in the skies, the great floods and sea life found on dry land. The Gods are fulfilling a prophecy, foretold by Goddesses worshiped by the people of *prophecy*. Mankind first worshiped Goddesses. The reign of these deities started when man started tool building and lived in small groups of 30-500 individuals. The Goddesses helped with childbirth, animal husbandry, and also started crop sharing that lasted till large Civilizations grew up, in areas of Africa, Asia Minor, East Asia, and India during and before the days of Sanskrit/Vedic Sanskrit. With the early trade routes across the Atlantic by barge, trade in food stuffs, hallucinogenic drugs, people, some animals and religious ideology, areas including South America, central and southern areas of North America, were part of the Goddess Deities areas of worship. The Goddess Deities prophesied their replacement with Gods and Demons, as societies would grow more war like and less propitiatory. The last of the great Goddess civilizations died with the Greek/Trojan War, The Amazonian female warriors were at their strongest in the days of the Trojan War. They overreached themselves by joining forces with the Greeks to destroy the Trojans. The Great Addas Ababa fell to invading warriors from the East, as large numbers of Amazonian warriors were in battle in and around the Mediterranean. The warriors left to guard the homeland were outnumbered, and the whole of the Goddess

Nation, encompassing Africa, including areas that would be known as: Egypt, Saudi Arabia, Iraq, Jordan, Syria, Jerusalem along The Nile River were annihilated.

And now we fly amongst monsters, beasts, Gods, Demons, and Dragons. The ***Child of Truth*** flys! ***She is The Mako***! The Mako flys through the mayhem of Gods and Demons striking out at each other. While the Earth is being tested by forces from the great Spaces above and beyond its location beneath the Orbits of Heavenly Bodies. The Gods and Goddesses are changing places, taking and giving up power. The Earth is being assaulted from the Heavens while facing changes from under the surface of the continental areas. We fly unhindered by the changes going on in, and above the Earth. The people that are moving on the Earth do not see us or all that have gathered to witness the flight of the Mako. The struggle of Man is not our concern; only that some of the very highly trained persons, may view our passing through drug induced visions, or Shamanistic practices of perception. Stories will travel the Globe of the Sky Demons, Dragons, Huge turtles, and what look like ***Cities of Light*** floating in the sky. Leading whole groups of God worshiping people to try many ways to ascend to the Heavens. Some try to fly, some travel to mountain tops, some build tall towers, and a very few try building a stairway to Heaven. All the Gods including Buddha, Allah, Jehovah, the Twelve Olympians, Zeus, Hara, Poseidon, Demeter, Athena, Apollo, Artemis, Ares, Aphrodite, Hephaestus, Hermes, Dionysus. Their parents Cronus and Rhea have Cities of Light, in the sky. Stairways are the way of Mankind to them. Both in legend and in spirituality. So, the Gods welcome Mankind's pursuit to ascend upwards on Heavens staircase.

13/06/16 23:00

I am the Fixer; I fly with the Mako, we now have the wings of Hell upon our back once again. It feels right to have these wings back. Heaven's wings are exceptionally formidable but lack the allure of flash that matches my ***Hellish*** personality. The Mako looks distinctively Brilliant dressed in *Hell's* wings! She is fucking beautiful, blackened armor, blackened wings, skin of milk, long golden hair, and Her eyes of Blue Diamond. I want to fuck her here as we fly! Flying over the *Hell* that is everywhere below, and all around us! The Mako only has eyes for the truth, but the *Ghost of Hell* in her head, will want to get fucked. What the fuck, lets fly to the Kunlun

Mountains, and find something to make her trip her success! Hell has found the space between us and the Earth below, to be the only place for it to tactically maneuver on us. The sky everywhere is full of flying beasts, dragons, Heaven's Angels and Gods from the far reaches of the universe. *Hell* has no power to fight these *Deities*. Hell will have to wait, "Fuck you Hell, Fuck you I yell!!" I fly down and rip Demons, and Hellhounds apart for shits and giggles. I fly straight at Hell's Angels and cut some to shreds! Some fight back, fuck you, I want to kill all of you! I'm the Fixer. I scream to the Mako, "Get down here, lets fuck these things up now!!" She flies down, the Ghost of Hell has taken a liking to the chance of killing some of these things, and maybe something else. The Mako spins, twists, flashes, appears and disappears. Demons, dragons, Hellhounds, and Heaven's Angels shredded! She screams when sending her sword through a Heaven's Angel or a Hell's Angel. Then surfs by standing on her shield upon Shyok River, "*The River of Death*".

We have flown out of Tibet and entered India, but in the times we now fly in, these countries are not established or named as yet. The people are different in language and teaching, but the Godhead government leaders are war like, and large civilizations do not exist yet. Surfing the River on her shield is an excellent way to chase these monsters. Some chase the Mako. I dive into the River moving under the surface of the water. We move as a group in formation, breaking only to engage in combat. The group of ***Eight Immortals***. Towards the Hindu Kush, and the Old Khmer mountain ranges. Also, what is now called *Uttar Pradesh*. As we move to the Uttar Pradesh, the River Ganges, & Yamuna, run together at the Allahabad, then the Ganges flows East. Towards the Kunlun, we see the lavish paradisiacal details of beauty; with gem like rocks, towering cliffs made of Jade and Jasper. Plants here are exotic, they have a bejewelled appearance. The lake of Gems lay at the base of these mountains. Deities such as Xiwangmu, Yushi, Tai di, and Sun Wukong have made this place their home. The mountains have seemingly Golden Ramparts that from an angle, and look like a huge castle, covered with Gemstones and bejewelled plants. Sanskrit called *Sailaraja*- The king of the mountains. This is what we will be called but now the Mako is seeking the truth buried here in the Kunlun, Hindu Kush, Caucasus Indicus and the western Himalayas Region.

28/06/16 22:00

The Hellish beasts drop away from us as we travel upriver to the lake of Jewels.

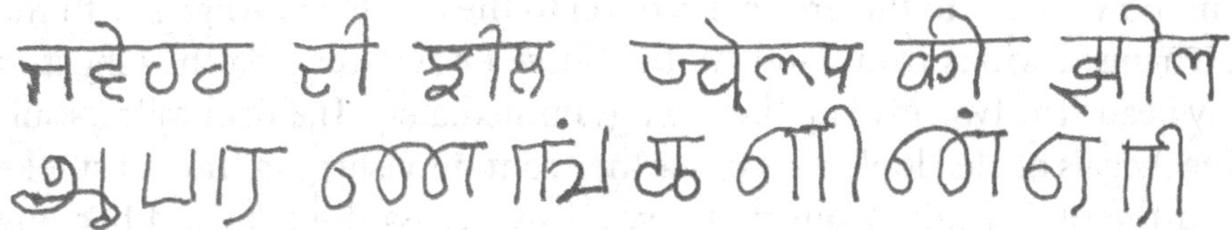

The water surface is calm and smooth. I move just below the surface without disturbing the water. The group of Angels above us move across the lake and break apart as we reach the Eastern edge of the shoreline. There are several large Headlands jutting out over the water, giving the cliffs and mountainous areas a hallucinatory dream quality. We Eight stand on a rocky shoreline, gaze upwards to the outcroppings of *"Jade & Jasper"* cliffs. Buttresses of rock support overhanging projections over Promontories that jut out into the water. The Mako looks everywhere, then flies to many of the outcroppings, one after another. Selects one and sits still, as if waiting for someone to advance on our position. Looking out across the water, I notice we have company. Dragons and Angels are flying towards us. Then I see Citys of Light hanging in the distant sky. All manner of beasts move and are moving beneath the water surface. There is also a gathering of mortals, to the North of our position. There are 10s of thousands of people. In the forefront are religious leaders and Royalty. They are of different cultures. Some *Punjabi, Japanese, Chinese, Arab, African, and Greek.* They are *Buddhist, Hindu, Amazonian, Muslim, Shinto.* Many people speak in *Vedic Sanskrit.* The language is beautiful to listen to and they are singing it to us. Some of the drug induced Shamans can see us! So, they sing to us!

The Uttarakhand, **Land of Gods**, The truth that the Mako seeks is before us now. The people that are making the long perilous trek up the *Shyok River*, though countryside that has been changing rapidly with the coming of the Gods. These people are not alone, more than 50 thousand of them have come, along with their Angels. It is truly a sight to see! Hundreds of thousands of Angels fly all around these people, above and below the earth. Along with some of their deities. I fly up to be with the Mako, I see why she is watching from this vantage point. The water is shimmering from fires burning all along the distant shoreline. The sky is filled with colors. In the far distance a volcano is filling the sky with a fiery glow, that pulses with convection.

I am the Mako, I have come here for a *truth* that has to be started here and now. I flash to the group. I motion to the two Hell's Angels with the exchanged wings from God. With a force known only by the Ghost in my head. The two, give up their wings immediately. The fixer follows suit. The Angels of Hell look amazing as they continuously emit trails of smoke, and the bluish mist from their eyes. I fly across the lake and become immersed in humanity; they can't see me as I move amongst them. Then I come to a group of people who are setting up a kind of hospital, mostly for pregnant women and those with broken bones. I look around me; the group of *Eight* are here. I look to the Fixer; his duality is admonished with my intent. I am the Mako! The truth is here and now! Angels from heaven begin to chant, as I ask them to provide me their shields. I hand shields to the group of eight.

Angels of Hell have never handled a shield before, things in Heaven are not in the *realm* of Hell. They struggle to grasp onto the shields. While Heaven's Angels seem totally out of place, having given up their shields! I fly above the ground; holding my shield up above my head, and then I strike it with my sword!! The shield immediately explodes!! The portal is destroyed the lightening bolt. Streaks of light radiate in all directions as the portal passes its power to me. The salt water in the shield is vaporized by the lightning bolt sword; the resulting steam is minute particles of Holy water that drift down upon the group of eight. They are holding the shields above their heads, so as to be protected from the Holy water. But not completely, I settle beside them. The holy water makes us visible to humanity. People fall to their knees; some stand and chant, some sing and move in a rhythmic dance. The crowd splits from many different places. The Shamanistic leaders move through the breaks in the crowd. They are beautiful, graceful and confident. They all are carrying a flower and a piece of fruit; they are Peach Blossoms, and the fruits are Golden Peaches. The religious leaders want to commune with us, offering the blossoms and fruit for our approval. I take the flowers and walk through the pregnant childbearing women giving them the blossoms. I then strike the ground and plant a seed from the peach I am holding. Mako: "This tree will grow to be Thousands of years old; it will provide fruit approximately every 6000 years that will give a mortal, immortality! That a group of thinkers and religious people may flourish in this region to have constant contact with the Gods and Deities! People here will call this the '*Peach Festival*', here, transformation from *Mortality*, to *Immortality*, will be possible!"

03/07/16 23:00

I watch the Mako as she strokes the ground and plants the peach seed. Unbelievably she starts to flicker, her blackened armor becomes translucent and then blackened then translucent. The wings of Heaven flash as if they are wings of Hell!! The Mako flashes and the Ghost of Hell in her, is all that is visible. The Hellish thing is also beautiful, and so Fucking Awesome. God's armor falls to the ground all around the Ghost of Hell. Suddenly the ground begins to shift in place, and the Diaphanous one appears! The brilliant light is striking as the mist of Holy water continues to fall, falling onto this the most Holy of All. God speaks through the fixer to the Mako. Fixer: "This truth you are seeking here is the most dangerous. You have an unbelievable ability to extract truths. I am powerless to stop you from this discovery; however, this truth seals your fate with Hell! I know that all we see is the Ghost of Hell, but I also know that the Mako is '*Between Gates*' now and can hear what this Ghost hears. Mako, uncover this truth! Do not let the ghost of Hell do this. The power of the *Truth Child* is more confident than this *Beast!*" The Ghost of Hell spreads the wings of Heaven screams and the Holy water spills upon the beast! Hellfire breaks out, and the beast is consumed as a bluish fog lifts from her. The armor begins to shimmer and glow, then it is translucent and finally changes to its original beauty, pure white. White as the snow on a frost covered mountain. Then more flashes as the Ghost of Hell burns completely from The Hellfire. The Mako returns to her wings, for a time, her beautiful body is completely naked before as all. Then the armor, God's pure love lifts up and is again clad upon her body. This angel of Heaven is now one with immortality.

The Ghost of Hell is now gone to once again be with Hell. The Mako is now a New Angel. The *Truth Child* is now with her because of this discovery, and the sealed fate by God and his covenant with Hell. The light dims and the Diaphanous one is gone. I look upon the Mako. She looks just as when first I laid eyes on her and froze her. Beautiful, strong, confident, and now a duality with The Holy spirit, and no longer the Ghost of Hell. Fixer: "Mako, what is the truth, what have you come here for? To plant a seed for mortals to dream of immortality? Have you come here to give new life a dream to cling onto? Have you come here to change the Ghost of Hell into the Truth Child?" The Mako walks around then glides toward me. She is not walking on this Earth! She is not here for us or them. The truth is not apparent to anyone but Herself, The *Truth Child*, and God. She bends down, reaches out, pulls a sword of lightning, and a portal of saltwater shield from nowhere!! She is an Angel of God once more. Mako: "Fixer, I am not of your realm anymore. I am a Heaven's Angel once more. I came here to discover a truth. Fixer you have come to here to be set free. I will show you the truth, the truth will set you free. I will be without your council for some time, as you explore your freedom. Whether or not we are once again together, will depend on you and your actions. I must take refuge here amongst these people and assist their assent to and from various Gods and deities, as well as the *Cities of Light*. While Demons roam the blood-soaked battle fields, amidst the Kayos of the Gods & Goddesses exchanging their roles. Are you ready Fixer? Are you ready, for your freedom?"

The Fixer flashes his wings, screams and Howls!! Fixer: "I am ready for anything! I am the Fixer, I have come here to be with you, to find the truth. I have come here to be with the immortals, and The Gods of the Earth. I have come here to correct mistakes of old. What truth have you that sets me free? What truth have you found here at the start of the Peach Festival; the immortal ground that we stand upon?" The Mako, in a grand gesture with her sword above her head points in all Four directions, as she speaks. Mako: "This land, the Land of the Gods. This land will keep the truth of mortality safe for thousands of years until the **End of Days**! This land will change one mortal every 6000 years, into an Immortal. Through the Peach Festival using the *elixir* derived by some shamanistic Medicine Man and his concubine, as for told by the Immortals that dwell here. These Immortals will need to replenish their immortality every 3000 years, by returning here to drink the elixir. Some of these immortals will create beasts and demons on Earth through their miss deeds, and chance meetings with the Ghost of Hell that once resided in me and now resides in a city far off to the west of here called Babylon. Fixer, the truth here is not the immortality to certain individuals, or the practice of the Peach festival in this land. It is the immorality of God himself! After I planted the seed, I left this place, I stood between the Gates of Heaven and the Gates Hell. I watched the Ghost of Hell change my body. I was able to understand how immortality works. The souls are created here on Earth and go through a series of trials. Some of these souls never leave the womb. Some have children, some are barren. God needs these souls to be immortal, and so does *Hell*. It's a business transaction, Between the Gates."

Mako: "However, the Immortals are a creation of God, not Hell! Fixer you are an Immortal, a creation of God not of Hell, you were trapped in Hell, part of a **Great Test** by both Heaven & Hell. Only, you used your power to heal and save a soul to free yourself! God gave you that power. Once freed, you became a rouge force that challenges The Christ and You then created me. I am the Mako, only envisioned by God himself, as a possibility of your freedom from Hell! Now your freedom from Serving the Mako will be The reason I must now Take refuge Here on Earth. Fixer, The Earth is like a tree, the seeds of souls are a testing ground for the immortality of Gods and Deities. They can be cloned or expanded at the same time, this way immortals can never challenge the Gods; as they, the Gods have a constant source of essence while the immortals cannot be cloned or reproduce. Thus, their essence is not transferable. It was through your *great test* in chains in a cell locked away in Hell, that God was able to trace a soul's essence through the mortal by testing clones of the ones set on, by you. Once freed, God then needed to create the Christ. And now you are free to challenge all the coming Gods, and also the duality, Christ, when he arrives on Earth. Fixer, you and I were reborn in Heaven, we Traveled to Hell where I slew The River Styx. I separated the dead lost souls from their *essence* and peeled off the poisonous river to expose the truth there. We then portaled to the Crossroads in Heaven, where the truth there was your own **will**, and the freedom that it brought you here. Now you can test your own immortality, chase that Ghost in Hell and challenge any duality that may confront you. I wish you God Speed and I wish to see you again at my side before I die on the banks of the River STYX!"

I am an Angel of Hell; I have been reborn in heaven. I have stood at the Crossroads in Heaven. I have been hunted by Hell and its Demons. I am now in the Land of the Gods on Earth with the Mako. As she now assumes her role as a duality without the Ghost of Hell. I Fly at her and scream! She stands motion less, I look into her eyes, she looks into mine. I feel her duality; it is much stronger than it was previously. I walk around her and through the group of eight. I stop at one of the two who followed us. I exchange wings with him. I dawn Heavens wings once more, they were given to me at the crossroads in Heaven when I received Free will.

I will wear them till time on Earth stops. I flash; I remerge over the Lake of Jewels. I flash I reemerge over Babylon; several Angels rise up from the portal under the city straight from Hell. They start to fly in circles around me. This is going to be an exercise in pure justice. They flash, I flash, I move between the gates of Heaven and Hell I reemerge where they were. They are now where I was, waiting for my return. They are more than a little angry and intend to change my position with Hell. I freeze them. I look into their minds. They are mostly vacant beings except the Ghost of Hell that was in the Mako. I hold them in a frozen state until the Angels are all on fire. Hellfire surrounds the group. I can kill them all here and now. Hell can't stop me these things are not capable of putting up a fight against me. I cause the Ghost to transplant into me once again where she was before I planted her into the Mako. I then steal one more ghost. I unfreeze the group there are six of them, four of them drift down. I fly and kill one of the vacant Angels! That's right, go to Hell!!

I turn to the other vacant Angel she is still on fire; I grab her and flash. We are in Hell. Hell moves a group of Angels and beasts towards us as we arrive. I freeze all of them; the vacant Angel is no longer on fire and is healing as I plant two Ghosts of Hell in her head! I look at her and I study the new duality, I let her see my duality, my pain my great test and the final escape and how Hell and Heaven hunted me. I am losing my grip on her as her duality begins to take hold, and her consciousness processes her new power: She breaks free and flies around Hell screaming and slashing at demons and all of the beasts in Hell!! Then she flies to me and reaches out. I hand her the sword I hold and the shield as well. We know instantly and we flash.

We reemerge in a place I was once when I stood on the shores of the Lake of Jewels with the Mako. Everyone is gone, the people, the Gods, the Dragons and *Cities of Light*. The place doesn't look the same either. It appears as though much time has passed by while I have been away in Hell. We must find the Mako, we must find the group of Eight. The Mako does not have to die on the shore of the STYX. The earth can have its final battle, but I have to change the outcome for Heaven and Hell with this new duality. The truths that are found can swing the balance in favor of Heaven. The stars can continue to shine on in the universe, and life can flourish into the future. I fly all around, the Angel of Babylon flies with me as we pass under the lake and over the huge stairway, this place is beautiful!

The Golden Ramparts, the beautiful Jade encrusted rock buttresses. All the plants, bejeweled, and the fog surrounding this mountainous enclave and the headlands. I can see fires burning in the distance and smoke drifting. Man has built cities in the area, and monks have moved into the mountains to start training new Religions of the Gods. The old Goddesses religions are gone. The Aryans are In India, early Taoism (Daoism) is spreading in China. Buddhism will soon find its way from the mountains here in the Himalayas, the mythical Kunlun, and the Land of the Gods. These people are using the local hallucinogenic plants and fungi to mix with peaches and apricots to experiment with immortality. The Silk Road will provide a whole external population with religion, amongst skilled shamanistic seers. Hell uses hallucinogens to produce the Demons and Angels it requires. So, it's required for Shamanistic people to see the immortals. Now with the use of an elixir they are trying to produce an immortal. Angels of Hell will mix with these people to produce societies who will live far beyond their time – 100s of years. Some of which will turn into monsters, vampires, werewolves, shape shifters, and later the Sumerians with Babylon and The Angels of Babylon, one of whom I fly with now. This whole vast area will produce more souls for Hell than were even imagined possible. Hell will grow exponentially leading to the great test where I was locked up for eternity.

Now we watch as a large procession of people, soldiers, religious elite, and royalty are migrating out of India (These are The Aryan). They will pass through the mountains of the Hindu Kush, and the Himalayas. Then along the Kunlun Shan, the Mekong into what will be Vietnam. Then north up the Xiang river.

Eventually, up the Yangtze to Shanghai, where they will follow ocean currents to distant islands and into Ancient Japan. These people will be the ones to follow while I seek the Mako. I fly to the mountain headlands and take in the sight. The numbers are staggering. Hundreds of thousands of people in groups of some thousands' at a time. Hundreds of thousands' of animals and millions of birds. All the while are the Angel's of people and the Angel's of Hell. This migration is just unbelievable, fires spread as they move, wild animals move with and alongside the groups. My Babylon's Angel accompanies me now while I fly down to be with the peoples and among the animals. The Mako seeks truths. I seek only freedom. I move amongst the people, animals and their Angels. The Angels here give way for us as we fly, their numbers don't mean anything to us. All Angels have a mission and cannot jeopardize their assignments to come into conflict with me. They cower and appear in a pusillanimous condition. The numbers of Angels here with humanity are truly multitudinous. Nevertheless, they all give way for us to travel with them. The Bitch from Hell flashes, as do I. We portal to the Far East coast. I am sure the Mako came this way to the ocean. Hell hunts her but can't keep track of her wear-bouts because of her new duality, minus the Ghost of Hell. And now I can't Fuck'n find her. However, I will, and that's why I brought this Bitch with me, she will find the Mako of that, I am sure. She flashes, I follow we step out into Heaven, I am not sure why she has come here, and I am sure this might be a mistake; however, this duality is devious.

This is just fucked up! I stepped through the bubble from a portal with wings from Heaven. Accompanied by a Babylonian Bitch from Hell into Heaven, onto one of the golden streets. Our bodies are streaming smoke trails, and we cannot touch the golden streets but that sparks and smoke drifts from our every step. Bells are ringing all around as Heaven's Angels are gathering in great numbers to watch our passing down the road. Souls flicker and dance by. Animals move on the grounds; rainbows appear in the sky as clouds pass and the sky turns dark in places. Stars and planetoids pass over. We continue to walk down the road. I am beginning to remember this place. This is the road I walked with the Mako as we moved towards the crossroads. I am beginning to feel the importance of this plan by the Hell's Angel at my side. She is going to use her duality to empathically possess the Mako's location from the positioning of the crossroads. Hell wants the Mako as much as I do. If anything can find her this Bitch from Hell can. She can't replace the Mako, she isn't as strong a fighter as the Mako is however, the duality of a Hell's Angel is a devious thing to possess, and here in Heaven, this will either work, or she will find out like I and the Mako did that God holds sway what goes down here. What a beautiful place, green grass like no other, flowers and butterflies, sparks of light, birds of all types, animals and rainbows. We walk on towards the crossroads, and then when we arrive from the direction of mission we find stepping out of a portal, the Trinity.

The Diaphanous speaks: "Stop Here! I am your God! You will stop here at the crossroads! I sense that you are here to seek The Mako, Hell has sent the two of you here. I however have not invited either of you here.

You can not gain anything here and she knows that." A rod of lightening points straight at the Bitch of Babylon. She smiles at God, she knows that the truth here, is in the Fixer. She screams and strokes the street with her sword, drawing a line on it. Smoke and a blue flame appear as she drags the sword. Fire is not possible here in Heaven. She is tempting God to strike her down, knowing full well he cannot. God does not care about her or me. He sends the golden bolt straight to her chest and speaks. God: "You will not challenge me here, or I will strike you down." The blue flame goes out, the sword is withdrawn. She flashes; she has no portal nor Heaven's wings to contend with. She reappears beside the transparent one she dances around him. He begins to flicker but stands his ground. She flashes and reappears beside the Christ. God launches his golden rod straight through her. She is impaled on the rod and cannot move but she screams and stabs her sword into the Christ and drops her shield onto the street. Christ reaches out, pulls the golden rod from the chest of the Angel of Hell, as he begins to flicker. A blue flame appears from his wound. The shield strikes the golden street, the portal disintegrates, this time pearls do not flood Heaven. This time sand pours out and continues to pour out. The light from God becomes unbearable to look at!

Then his flash envelops the Christ, the source of sand, and both disappear. The Bitch screams and kicks sand, smoke, sparks and small blue flames lash out. She flashes and reappears beside me. Then God produces another rod and dims his brilliance. "The Fixer has his Will; the Crossroads are not the place for you! You're spreading the *sands of time* here will be your undoing. I will not give into Hell; you will have to locate the Mako on your own." This is an Angel of Hell, and this Bitch is a duality, Hell sent it here to locate the Mako, and she don't give a fuck if God can kill her, and me. She is going to play a game, and the stakes are high. In her mind, she deals the cards picks them up, shuffles them, and then redeals. Every card she deals out is: Fuck you, Fuck you, and Fuck him. Then she finds the Queen of Diamonds, she screams at God and says "Hell sent me here to lay claim on the Mako, I have a card in my mind, and you know what it is. I want to fill that card. Hell doesn't give a Fuck about the Pearl Nautilus, the Fixer, or you either!! If the Mako isn't stopped and stripped of the truth and her soul! So, let's play for real, I will play my card, let's see if you call my bluff. Come on God what the Fuck kind of card have you got to trump this?!" She flashes and steps out of a portal high in Heaven. Slowly a card from a deck of Tarot Cards drifts down to the golden crossroads.

It's the Queen of Diamonds! The **_Hell's_** Bitch freezes everything. Heaven's Angels are in exceptionally large numbers around the group, **_and now_** all of them are frozen! The Christ has been removed and so cannot absorb the pain; God's armor will fall!!

11/07/16 23:00 DCA

I look at her; I move close to her, she is frozen. Impossible! Fucking impossible, I fucked up this Bitch for sure! She has frozen everything in Heaven for as far as I can see. She planned this before we even got here for fuck sakes. She is not even in her head. This is fucked up. The Transparent one is flashing and flickering, the diaphanous one is giving off a brilliance. that is threatening to kill everything in Heaven. As I look at her, I am looking at a vacant shell, she is not in there. Both of her Ghosts of Hell are moving from one Heaven's Angel to another just as fast as they can. God's armor is raining down to the ground in Heaven. Angels are drifting down onto the ground naked, and they are crying! God's brilliance goes out and the one that walks on water returns to God's side. The Bitch turns and looks at me, she has returned. God's Angels are everywhere, this looks like a total disaster. She grins, she rakes me with a clawed hand, I scream, spin away and deal her a wound that won't heal. She doesn't realize my power, or she wouldn't have done that. She drops to the golden street. She vacates the dying Bitch and moves into a Heaven's Angel right in front of me. Her old body is a smoldering carcass. God touches her; the wings disappear. That's it she is totally helpless now. She is trapped in the mind of an angel with no way to teleport or vacate. "Hell needs you to complete the mission!" I reach into her mind; she has found the Mako. God gave her up to the Ghost of Hell that I added to her. I pull the Ghost. God immediately beheads the Angel; I watch as a spark lifts to the heavens. I watch a black smoke drift as she is taken to Hell. Finally, I know where the Mako is.

I am still trying to take in what has happened, as God points a golden staff at me. God: "Fixer, you brought her here. You will take that smoldering carcass with you when you leave! You will only to be allowed in heaven again if you return with the Mako. Too many things have happened here because of your unexpected arrival with this Babylonian Angel from Hell. I cannot forgive you for what has happened. Spilling the **_sands of time_** in Heaven caused time to pass without me present on Earth. When she speared the one that walks on water, my son on Earth died at the hand of a Centurian named Longinus. I had to give up the Mako in order to save my son; and clean up the sands of time before anymore terrible things happened on Earth without me. And now you know that I have killed a Heaven's Angel in Heaven to stop a Hell's Angel from escaping with a Ghost of Hell bound to kill the Mako. All the while the Angels all around have all lost their armor from the freeze. All of this will end when you are on the front line of the battle of Evermore. I assure you; you will be there with all of us. These things you do here cement your place in Hell and in Heaven. Go now, find the Mako, and tell Her all that has and will happen. Fore, the sands of time have not affected Her. Let Her find all the truths she seeks and then bring her home to Heaven, one last time before she goes to Hell. The truths she seeks are for Heaven & Earth."

Hell will have to wait! As the Fixer I stride while smoke drifts from me. I gather her the carcass. I look at all the Angels, I make my promise to God. I flash and step into, and out of a portal into Hell.

EPILOGUE

I shine a light in the night.

I place the full moon in the sky at night to control your passion. The ebb and flow contains a period of freedom to which your spirit refreshens. The light that shines from the moon dims as it becomes smaller. And in the night, you may become lost. So, without knowing, I place the stars in the heavens in fixed places to give you reference. I place moving bodies in the stars to encourage you to move. The ones that come and go in your life, friends, and family they also shine a light in your life. Some fixed, some moving. But all must pass from sight. When they pass, the light from their life leaves your mind. I then take their light and add it to the stars in the heavens. So many you cannot count. So many you don't know. They are there to light your way even in the darkest night. Alas, you may find a night when the light cannot pass through the clouds. This is when you must depend on your faith. In the darkest night you look into the heavens and no light appears. Faithfully, you know that in the heavens beats the heart of one that loves you more than any man. With that love you may find peace and it will light up your soul.

Questions: 1-12:

- Answer: Within days of ending my 30 + year marriage, I was discussing the situation with a close friend and extended family member. I began to relive my life and buried memories. I became overtaken by the presence of my deceased son.

- The story spans 25000, years. A mistake made by the gods starts a chain of events leading to the war of evermore. The escape of a God locked up creates a new God and together they find the truth.

- The central theme is, good and bad are opposite forces. These forces are never in balance. One is always threatening to overpower the other. Ultimately, the death of one leads to the death of the other, they are codependent.

- This book takes place on earth, in the heavens, and in Hell.

- The main characters are The Fixer, and The Mako.

- The Fixer is the most powerful Hell's angel, a literal God.

- The Mako is God produced by Heaven and the virtual power of the mind of Hell. The Mako is a Japanese name. Meaning (loosely) The Child of Truth. The Two "Gods" become codependent. The fixer wants to undo the mistakes of the Gods & Goddess. The Mako wants to expose all the truths of deception made by all the Gods.

- This story has truly been an escape for my mind. There is so much deception in the world today. We live in a time on the brink of Armageddon. It is a universal theme amongst all to want to escape the chains that bind us, and to come face to face with the truth of our beliefs.

- Today's society is watching too much TV, too much video, and playing too may games. We need to use our minds more to be creative, empower others, and build memories based on skillful achievements. Today is becoming truly a throwaway society. We are throwing away our lives on everything.

- I write in the first person; therefore, the reader gets to be right there amongst every situation. That's empowerment. The readers mind gets to see how things are, I leave enough holes in description to allow the reader to use his/her imagination. That's creativity. I don't use gross language to describe events, allowing the reader to decide how much is enough. That's a life skill ability.

- The story is one derived from a life event that's all engrossing. The loss of a life not lived. I took the story from the passing of a child this is not a made-up event. I created a story from a story of extreme pain, heart break, and loss.

- I want readers to be shaken up; I want them to go for a journey in their mind. I want them to experience what is all around, and what has been, and what can be. Finally, I want the reader to find some truth in their beliefs.

- I believe that the story was told to me while I was with my infant son in ICU. Soon after birth he was terminal moved to ICU, 15 hours later he passed. His mother wanted no name or funeral. I was devastated. At the time I couldn't handle the loss, or the story he gave. For years I couldn't discuss the event with my spouse I married later in life. With the separation freshly happening, I felt the presence of the spirit and could smell the ICU. The spirit told me to draft the story, as I now had the life experience to do so. I did it, I wrote it.

- From the Epilogue: "I place the full moon in the night sky to control your passion. The ebb and flow contains a period of freedom to which your spirit refreshens.

STUDY NOTES

Fuyan Cave Dao County
Hunan

Bagua - 8 symbols. 八 卦
        8 Trigrams

daoist cosmology

yin or yang

taiji taijiquan wu xing

4	9	2
3	5	7
8	1	6

magic square.
qi - natural energy

Bagua

Qian Dui Li Zhen Xun Kan Gen Kun

Sixiang taiyang Shaoyin Shaoyang Taiyin

Liangyi Yang Yin taiji

64 hexagrams - (chessboard)
wu-wei
School of Yin Yang.

Taoism (Daoism) Tao means way, path
                 Principle
Chan (Zen) Buddhism, feng shui, qigong

56

Japan - early people - Jōmon - 21000 years ago.

Okinawan | Wang Mu. controlls plagues and evil spirits. Motherly
         | figure to all gods of heaven.
Shinto - | Fabled Garden of the Western Paradise - Kunlun Mountains
Kami-no-michi | Tibet and Xijiang.
Amaterasu - Shining in heaven | Kunlun range - part of the
                              | Silk Road. - China - Persia

The Kunlin mountians / Uttar Pradesh.

The Hindu Kush Mountian Range

Old Khmer (Old Cambodian

Sanskrit - Sailarāja kings of the mountian.

Trans - Gangetic Indra.

Sailendra Thalassocracy

The Kunlin is lavished with in paradisaical detail
Gem like rocks, towering cliffs of jasper or jade.
exotic jeweled plants bizarrely formed and colored
fungi and the Eight Imortals visiting with.
Xi Wangmu & Yu Shi Sun Wukong Tai Di
with golden ramparts. The lake of Gems.

Peaches produce Imortality every 6000 yrs.
The gods must drink an elixer made from peaches every 3000 yrs.
A peach with a leaf attached symbolizes the union of the heart a tounge
hence - truth.
Moon goddess Legend of Hou-yi Chang-e and Xiwang Mu's peaches.

The Golden Peaches of Samarkand

The kingdom of Samarkand.
Seeds, bark and leaves contain low levels of cyanide. Therapeutic
for cancer. Powerfull dose of Vitamin A.

Encyclopedia of Shinto - Kojiki - Okamuzumi.
Izanagi, Izanami, Yomi, Japan
India - Hindu Insani, Iswara
Brahma & Vishnu
Tree of Heaven, Cosmic Tree. Karma Tree.
Ngadu-tree trunk.
Oedeypoor, Rajputana
Rajput - Gehlote - Sessodian clans. Iswara and Isani.
Mahadera - Iswara - tutelary divinity of Rajpoots in Mewar
"Gehlote adoration" Annals, Antiquities of Rajasthan
Saka - Sassanian - Sila roots of the royal myths of Indian
and Japanese tribes. Marrage of Inanna and Dumuzi.
A Hymn of Sumer. A Tricontinental Nexus. Anatolia
Indus Valley.
Origin of the Aryan in India and their Migration to Ancient Japan.

東南アジア研究年報, 52.

pp. 21-28; 2011 | Similarities and common Saka - Sassanian - Sila
                  roots of the royal myths of Indian and Japanese tribes.
Xiwang Mu. | Shikome. August Male.

North Pakistan - Budapest.   The Eurasian Steppe, Mongolia.
A bride in China carries peach blossoms.
The peach - symbol of longevity, femal sexuality, purity & truth
        - is the yin

Tarim Basin - Bronze Age.
The Peach as a Kami. a Mother goddess Momotaro, Kamishibai.com
Shen, Phallus, Persian Apple.

REFERENCES

- Readers Digest

- *Atlas of the World*; ISBN # 0-89577-264-7
  All names of Countries, provinces, rivers, and lakes, I located in
  this book for spelling and geological location.

- *The New Webster Encyclopedic Dictionary*
  This book was indispensable for spelling, tense, usage, and
  meaning of various words. Also, used in the looking up of some
  Gods & Goddesses.

- *Wikipedia.org*
  Where I looked up names of deities as given to me by the ghost in
  my head.

This book and its contents are a work of fiction.
No claim is made by its author to real events or any timeline.

An Editorial Review of Hellish Inc.

"A visceral and unrelenting journey into the eternal struggle between Heaven and Hell, Hellish is a novel that refuses to be ignored. This dark fantasy epic weaves a harrowing tale of fallen angels, celestial warriors, and the tortured souls caught in between, creating a world as haunting as it is mesmerizing. From the opening pages, the novel grips readers with its raw intensity.

> **It is not a book for the faint of heart, but for those willing to embrace its nightmarish beauty, it is an unforgettable read.**

The protagonist, a tormented Hell's Angel known as the Fixer, is a compelling force-both a product of Hell's fury and a creature seeking redemption in ways neither Heaven nor Hell could have foreseen. His internal struggle, torn between hatred and longing for salvation, adds layers of depth that elevate the narrative beyond standard dark fantasy tropes. The writing is unapologetically vivid, at times poetic, at times brutal, immersing readers in scenes of celestial warfare and the psychological torment of its characters. The depiction of Heaven's luminous warriors and Hell's monstrous legions is striking, painting a world where the battle between good and evil is anything but clear-cut.

Themes of duality-love and hate, salvation and damnation, chaos and order-are explored with a philosophical weight that lingers long after the last page is turned. While the novel's ambition is commendable, the narrative's complexity may prove challenging for some readers. The experimental structure, intense descriptions, and deep internal monologues require a patient and engaged audience. However, for those willing to delve into its depths, Hellish offers a uniquely rewarding experience—a tale that is equal parts horror, theology, and existential reflection.

Bold, poetic, and fiercely original, Hellish is a tour de force in dark fantasy, appealing to fans of Paradise Lost, The Sandman, and The Divine Comedy, It is not a book for the faint of heart, but for those willing to embrace its nightmarish beauty, it is an unforgettable read."